W9-DIV-482

# THE CABLE GUY

COLUMBIA PICTURES

A BERNIE BRILLSTEIN/BRAD GREY PRODUCTION    A LIGHT/MUELLER FILM CORP. PRODUCTION    A BEN STILLER FILM

STARRING JIM CARREY MATTHEW BRODERICK "THE CABLE GUY" LESLIE MANN GEORGE SEGAL AND JACK BLACK

MUSIC BY JOHN OTTMAN

FILM EDITOR STEVEN WEISBERG

PRODUCTION DESIGNER SHARON SEYMOUR

DIRECTOR OF PHOTOGRAPHY ROB COHEN

CO-PRODUCER MARC GURVITZ    EXECUTIVE PRODUCER LOU HOLTZ, JR.    WRITTEN BY LOU HOLTZ, JR.    PRODUCED BY ANDREW LICHT AND JEFFREY A. MUELLER AND JUDD APATOW

DIRECTED BY BEN STILLER

EXECUTIVE PRODUCERS BRAD GREY · BERNIE BRILLSTEIN

PG-13 PARENTS STRONGLY CAUTIONED
Some Material May Be Inappropriate for Children Under 13

VISIT "THE SONY PICTURES ENTERTAINMENT SITE AT http://www.sony.com

# THE CABLE GUY

A NOVEL BY **HARRIET GREY**

BASED ON THE MOTION PICTURE WRITTEN BY **LOU HOLTZ, JR.**

St. Martin's Paperbacks

THE CABLE GUY

Copyright © 1996 Columbia Pictures Industries, Inc. All rights reserved.

Cover artwork copyright © 1996 Columbia Pictures Industries, Inc. All rights reserved.

All rights reserved. No part of this book may be used or reproduced in any manner whatsoever without written permission except in the case of brief quotations embodied in critical articles or reviews. For information address St. Martin's Press, 175 Fifth Avenue, New York, N.Y. 10010.

ISBN: 0-312-96082-4

Printed in the United States of America

St. Martin's Paperbacks edition / June 1996

10  9  8  7  6  5  4  3  2  1

# THE CABLE GUY

# Chapter One

The television had a twenty-seven-inch screen, closed captioning, a universal remote, and every other feature the discriminating viewer could want. It was big, it was sleek, it was *cutting-edge*.

Steven Kovacs stood in the middle of the empty living room in his brand-new apartment, impatiently flipping channels on the remote control box. Nothing but snow and the faint outlines of indistinguishable figures showed on the screen, and the sounds of static and white noise were deafening. Every time Steven changed the channel, a new ghostly, wavering image would appear. No matter how many times he got up and adjusted the antenna, he still couldn't get any decent reception. Yesterday he had maxed out his credit card on this television, and so far, the thing was useless.

Maybe the hypercritical salesman in the electronics department was right, and Steven's not signing up for the extended three-year warranty the store offered had been a terrible mistake.

"So where's the cable guy already?" he said through his teeth.

Steven was thirty years old, with short brown hair, and so clean-cut that he probably could have been the poster child for the Boy Next Door Contest. He looked at his watch and sighed heavily. Somehow it seemed to be one of the rules of being an adult in America that no matter what time the cable company said they were going to show up, they were always *hours* late. He had promised that he would be sitting patiently in his apartment between eight A.M. and six P.M.—no matter what—but the endless wait was starting to drive him crazy.

"I can't believe it," Steven said grimly to himself. "This is ridiculous."

Not that he had limited emotional resources—but, as far as he was concerned, a life without television was an empty life. Especially since his girlfriend, Robin, had just dumped him. She had claimed that they just needed to spend a little time apart, and "re-evaluate" things, but he was the one who had had to go to all the trouble of finding a new apartment, signing a lease, and hiring movers and everything.

To say nothing of being forced to live without cable for *hours* now.

The new apartment was nice, even though he didn't want to live here. The building dated back to the fifties, and there were lots of fancy architectural details like gargoyles and wainscotting. Since Steven worked in real estate development, he tended to notice these things. Sometimes, he even *appreciated* them.

Instead of lying around worrying about why he didn't have cable yet, he should probably start unpacking some of the boxes that were strewn all over the place, but he didn't really have the energy. Pointlessly pushing buttons on his remote control seemed like the most ambitious project he could handle right now.

He paced back and forth restlessly, and finally wandered out to the box-crowded kitchen. Behind him, the movers lugged a heavy sofa into the living room.

Should he go in and *sit* on the couch? Would that accomplish anything? Maybe he should just call his best friend, Rick, and complain bitterly about his lot in life for a while. Yeah, *that'd* kill some time until the cable guy took it upon himself to show up.

He looked around until he located the telephone underneath a pile of unpacked sweaters and then dialed the local television newsroom where Rick worked.

"Hello, Rick Legatos please," he said to the switchboard receptionist who answered the call.

It took a few minutes, but finally Rick picked up.

"Hey, it's me," Steven said.

"How's the move going?" Rick asked, having to shout over the noise of the busy newsroom. Behind him, on one of the closed-circuit televisions, an anchorman sat at his desk and fixed his hair as he waited to go on the air. A bright yellow graphic running along the bottom of the screen read SAM SWEET TRIAL UPDATE.

"Horrible," Steven grumbled, as he opened a box of dishes that was clearly marked KITCHEN, that the movers had inexplicably decided to put in the living room. "The cable guy is missing in action. Apparently he's going to be here sometime between eight A.M. and my death."

Rick laughed. "Oh, so it's going good?"

"Oh yeah," Steven said wryly. "It's going terrific."

"Glad to hear it." Then Rick paused. "You haven't called Robin, have you? Please tell me you didn't call her."

Not that Steven was feeling very sorry for himself and blaming his girlfriend for all of his current troubles—but yeah, he was blaming her for everything. "No, I'm 'giving her space,'" he said sarcastically, mimicking the same tone she had used during their last, very tense, conversation. He shook his head as he opened a box and saw some framed pictures of himself with Robin. In one, the two of them were lounging on a beach in San Juan; in another, they were standing arm-in-arm on the porch of his parents' summer cabin in the mountains; in a third, they were waltzing at their friend Billy's wedding reception. In *all* of the pictures, they looked very happy together.

Steven stared at the series of photographs, trying to decide whether to put them up on his new mantelpiece. Finally, he sighed and put them back in the box. For now, it would be a lot easier—and less depressing—just to start unpacking his books and CDs. "I can't believe she's doing this," he said into the telephone.

"You never should have asked her to marry

you," Rick answered. "You're the mad smotherer."

Didn't women usually complain that guys
didn't *want* commitment? So much for all of
those magazine articles that he would, of
course, never be caught dead reading. "All she
had to do was say no," Steven said. "She
didn't have to kick me out." Now he looked
down unhappily at the frying pan he had just
taken out of a KITCHEN box. "I feel like Felix
Unger."

Rick sighed. "You forced her to evaluate the
relationship. If you hadn't proposed, she
would never have realized how unhappy she
was."

Well, *there* was an optimistic point of view.
"I don't want to talk about it," Steven said,
dropping the frying pan back into the box and
taping it shut. Time to think about something
more cheerful. He was just going to have to
rise above the fact that he had a broken heart.
"So, what time are you going to come by?"

"Sorry, I can't," Rick told him cheerfully.
"I'm working double shifts the rest of the
week."

He was on his own—bereft, even—and his
best friend wasn't going to come over and
help him through all this? "It's my first night
here," Steven said, making sure to throw an

extra little note of pathos into his voice. "Don't do this to me." .

"The other camera guy pulled out his back," Rick explained. "Besides, I spent the last two weeks with you on my couch. Isn't that enough?"

Well, yeah, they had had kind of a lot of "togetherness" lately. Steven waved at the movers, who were just coming in with a breakfast table and chairs, and motioned for them to carry the furniture into the kitchen. "Fine, fine," he said, going out of his way to sound deeply wounded this time. "Don't worry about me. I'll be *just fine.*"

"You finished?" Rick asked.

Steven thought about that. "Actually, I think I'm good for another thirty seconds of whining."

Rick laughed. "Spare me, okay? One piece of advice, though," he added, before hanging up. "Slip the cable guy fifty bucks, he'll give you the movie channels for free."

Steven frowned. It might be nice to be the kind of person who walked on the wild side, but generally, he had always made a habit of playing by the rules. "I couldn't," he said hesitantly, although the idea was pretty tempting. "I'm not good at that stuff. I mean, what if he says no? I'll feel like an idiot."

"*None* of them say no, believe me," Rick as-

sured him. "I'll talk to you later, okay? You'll
be fine!"

Doubtful, at best. "Okay," Steven answered
and hung up.

He stood in the living room indecisively for
a few seconds and then looked at his watch.
The cable guy was so late that he probably
wasn't going to show up at all today.

For lack of a better idea, he continued unpacking. Steven was very neat and efficient, so
he worked his way methodically across the
room. Now that he thought about it, Robin *had*
called him "Felix" sometimes, but he wasn't
going to take that personally. No way. It
was—a coincidence, that's all.

By two-thirty, he had given up on the cable
guy. Digging around through one of the
KITCHEN boxes stacked in the bedroom, he
found a roll of aluminum foil. He peeled off
two long pieces of the foil and crumpled them
around the ends of the antenna on his television. Then he changed a few channels, but
there was still nothing but snow and white
noise.

"Great," he said through his teeth. "Oh, this
is just great."

Completely frustrated, he ripped the foil
from the antenna and threw it away.

He unpacked for about another hour, finishing up by hanging a clock on the kitchen wall.

It read: *3:20. Great.* Business hours would be over soon. He decided to go lie on his couch for a while and stare at the ceiling. Somehow, he just wasn't able to fill his day without cable.

"Where *is* he?" Steven asked aloud.

Unsurprisingly, no one answered.

Lying down was pretty boring, so after a few minutes, he got up and started pacing back and forth. Every so often, he would stop, stare at his watch, and mutter under his breath about how much he hated the cable company and was going to give up television forever. He would devote the rest of his life to reading literary classics.

Maybe.

At four-thirty, he made himself a ham and cheese sandwich, which he ate standing up at the counter in his kitchen. It had been such a long time that he had been on his own that he couldn't help feeling really lonely. So far, life in his new apartment was a parody of an unhappy bachelor's existence—and he wasn't enjoying a single second of it.

Even though he knew it was an extremely bad idea to give in to this particular temptation, he reached for the telephone and dialed Robin's number. After two rings, her—formerly *their*—answering machine picked up.

"Hi, this is Robin," her familiar, soft voice said. "Please leave a message. If you are trying to get Steven, he can now be reached at 555-0199."

Steven sighed and hung up before the beep. The finality in her voice hadn't done much to whet his appetite, but he picked up what was left of his sandwich and forced himself to keep eating.

Another hour passed, and the cable guy still hadn't shown up. Steven was so bored that he had started doing sit-ups in the middle of the living room. He *hated* doing sit-ups, but he couldn't think of anything better to do.

He was about to start on push-ups when he noticed that it was almost seven.

"Forget it," he said to himself. Obviously, the cable guy wasn't going to show up today. In fact, he was probably *never* going to show up. "Idiots."

He got up and headed for the bathroom. Taking a shower would kill a little time, and then he might be able to think of something interesting to do.

The water pressure in this apartment seemed to be pretty decent, and he adjusted the heat until it was exactly the way he liked it. While the water was running, he dug a thick towel out of a duffel bag in his bedroom, and got undressed. Then he climbed underneath the shower and tried to release some tension by letting the stream of hot water engulf him.

He had just lathered up his hair with shampoo when there was a knock on the door.

"Cable Guy!" a voice yelled from the hallway.

Naturally. Just when he had started to relax a little. "Oh *great*," he said and ducked his head underneath the water to wash off most of the soap. Some of it got in his eyes, and he yelped, trying to rub it away with his towel.

Then he jumped out of the shower, soaking wet, and grabbed a bathrobe. He raced out of the bathroom, leaving a trail of soapy water across the floor.

"Wait! Don't leave!" he yelled as he ran towards the front door. In his current state of romantic despair, he would never survive an entire *night* without television. "I'm here! I'm here!"

"Cable Guy!" the officious voice was still shouting between forceful knocks. "Cable Guy!"

Steven looked through the peephole just in time to see the Cable Guy walking away. Quickly, he threw the door open to stop him.

"Hey, wait!" he yelled.

The Cable Guy turned back and gave him a compact, toothy smile. "Well, look who decided to show up," he said. "I was just gonna go collect my retirement pension." He was wearing a clean white jumpsuit and sounded extremely confident, despite the fact that he spoke with a slight lisp. Even though he was tall and broad-shouldered, the lisp gave him a childlike quality.

"You were supposed to be here four hours ago," Steven said accusingly.

"Was I?" the Cable Guy lisped, holding a clipboard in one hand and a heavy box of tools in the other. "So *I'm* the tardy one. Good to know."

"Yes," Steven said, although it was hard to maintain his outrage and dignity when he was dripping wet and wearing nothing but a flimsy bathrobe. "I had to go to the Bed 'n Bath place, but now it's closed."

The Cable Guy looked at him without blinking and then spun around to leave. "All right then. Maybe I shouldn't have come at all . . . jerk!"

Steven couldn't help gasping, and the Cable Guy spun back with a wide smile.

"I'm just joking," he said. "Let's do this."

Without waiting to be invited, the Cable Guy marched right into the apartment with his toolbox. Then he paused to look around the room.

"Oh, the old McNair place," he said and then shook his head. "Wow. I never thought they'd get the carpets clean after what happened here."

Steven didn't like the sound of that, and he took a step back. "What happened?" he asked uneasily.

The Cable Guy didn't answer right away. "They had a lot of cats," he said finally.

Steven glanced down at his bare feet on the carpet, and couldn't help cringing slightly. He was curious, but maybe he would rather *not* know any more details about the former tenants' way of life.

The Cable Guy looked around some more. "Hey, this could be a cool pad," he said, then got back to business by taking out a small postcard and handing it to Steven without even turning to look at him. "Here is a comment card. Please mail it in when I'm done."

Steven skimmed the short list of quality of service questions written on the back of the card. "These go to your boss?"

The Cable Guy frowned and shook his head. "No, they go to *me*," he said, as though Steven were one of the most foolish people he had ever met. "I'm a perfectioniss—perfectioniss—" He couldn't get the word out right because of his lisp, and he tried a third time. "Perfectioniss . . . *t*." He nodded, looking pleased with himself. "Now then. Let's take a look at what we're dealing with here."

The Cable Guy started walking around the room with his hands out, sensing the space.

"So your lady kicked you out," he remarked conversationally as he drilled into the wall and plaster dust flew everywhere.

Steven blinked, startled by that. Was he wearing a sign on his back that said "I'VE BEEN DUMPED" or something? "What makes you say that?" he asked.

The Cable Guy shrugged and kept drilling. "In preparing your service," he said formally, "I noticed you were previously wired across town at 1268½ Chestnut. Last week, the billing was transferred to one Robin Harris." He shrugged again. "Smells like heartbreak to me, big guy."

Like it was any of his business? "I really don't want to talk about it with you," Steven said stiffly. "Could you please just install my cable? I'm going to get dressed."

The Cable Guy waved that aside, not even hearing the criticism. "Suit yourself. No sweat off my sack back."

Steven walked into the hallway towards the bedroom, and after a minute, the Cable Guy hustled after him.

"Hey, I'm going to go to the hallway, so I can access the floorboards," he said. "Don't be spooked if you hear someone crawling underneath you."

Steven shrugged. "Okay, whatever."

"And put on a bathing suit," the Cable Guy suggested, "'cause you'll be channel surfing in no time!" He laughed heartily and pulled the trigger on his drill twice to punctuate his joke.

Steven nodded to humor him and escaped into his room to get dressed.

After waiting all of those hours to get his cable hooked up, now he just wanted this guy to hurry up and *leave* already.

# Chapter Two

Once the cable had been hooked up, the Cable Guy turned on the television to check his work. He was nothing if not a cable purist. The box was already tuned to Court TV, and one of their reporters, Rikki Klieman, was broadcasting from the studio. The Cable Guy stepped back, examining even the tiniest details of the reception with trained and intensely critical eyes. While he was at it, he studied the reporter's on-camera skills, too.

"So ends day fifty-four of the trial of former child star Sam Sweet, who has been accused of shooting his twin brother, Stan, in cold blood," she said into the camera. "The twins were stars of the hit sitcom *Double Trouble*, which aired from 1977 until 1984."

The report then cut to a video montage, which showed several photographs of Sam Sweet and his twin brother at various ages in rapid succession. In each one, they both looked cloyingly adorable, with guileless eyes and big, fake showbiz smiles.

Next came a cast photo of the sitcom *Double Trouble,* which included the ubiquitous Conrad Janis—who had also played the single father in *Different Strokes*—as the twins' father. After that, there was a brief, staggeringly unfunny, clip from an episode of *Double Trouble*, including lots of canned studio laughter, followed by a final shot of Sam Sweet being led out of a police car in handcuffs.

The videotape ended there, and the camera went back live to Rikki Klieman, who was still looking solemn behind the anchor desk in the Court TV studio.

"Life wasn't sweet after the cancellation of their program," she reported. "Hollywood chewed them up and spit them out. A frustrated Sam turned to petty larceny, while his more impressionable brother, Stan, fell in with a fringe cult called The Brotherhood of Friends."

The Cable Guy shook his head in dismay, watching all of this.

"Reduced to tabloid fodder, a fury was

growing inside of Sam," Rikki Klieman went on gravely. "A burning need to be recognized as an individual, not a person famous for having an identical twin." She paused. "A need that took the form of four shotgun blasts on the night of November fourteenth. And so today, his attorneys continue the unusual defense of . . . 'Twin Envy,' also known as 'Twin Stress Syndrome.' "

Steven came back into the living room, fully dressed in an old sweatshirt, faded jeans, and sneakers. "How's it going?" he asked.

The Cable Guy held up one finger as if to say "quiet," his eyes never leaving the television for a second. "Guilty, guilty, guilt-freakin'-tee," he said. "I hope this guy gets what's coming to him."

The Sam Sweet trial. No matter where Steven found himself these days, someone was always talking about that stupid trial. But he decided not to pursue this particular conversation any further. After all, it wasn't as though he and the Cable Guy were forming some sort of *relationship* here and he had to put in any serious effort beyond simply being cordial. He glanced around the room, and then did a double take.

"Hey! What happened?" he demanded.

While he had been getting dressed, the Cable Guy had taken it upon himself to redecorate the room in a way which made it impractical for anything *other* than watching television. He had moved the television up onto the stairs, blocking the entrance into the living room. On top of that, all of the furniture was now facing the television, making it impossible for people to have any sort of normal conversation.

"Despite my best efforts, the arrangement of your major appliances and your furniture was causing some noisy pics and hum bars in your reception," the Cable Guy explained dryly, although most of his concentration was still directed towards Rikki Klieman's report. "I moved a few things. Cleared it right up. Is that cool?"

Steven was shocked by how horrible his living room looked, but he decided to take a non-confrontational attitude on this one. There was no point in hurting this guy's feelings. "I . . . guess so," he said.

"You programmed?" the Cable Guy asked.

Steven gave him a blank look.

The Cable Guy nodded wisely. "Thought as much. Then let me slave your remotes."

He picked up Steven's various remote control boxes, punched in a complicated series of electronic commands with dramatic flair, and pointed them at each other. As he held them together, he made a face as though their power was surging through him.

"Oooh," he said, making his entire body shudder. Then he stopped long enough to wink at Steven. "Maybe we should leave."

Yeah. Right. "So," Steven said, trying to keep the conversation purely professional. "After this, I'll only need one remote for everything?"

"You know you're pretty good at this," the Cable Guy remarked cheerfully. "You could be a cable guy yourself." Once the remotes were programmed, he set them down on the coffee table. "Now let me check your levels."

Levels? What levels? Steven frowned.

With amazing alacrity, the Cable Guy adjusted the color setting, sound controls, closed captioning, and other features on the television set until it was functioning at the very top of its capabilities. Then he clicked through all of the channels, zipping past a music video, a documentary on Hitler, Oprah Winfrey, a group of starving children in Third World countries, Barney, and back to Court TV.

"All righty," the Cable Guy said with great satisfaction, and dropped the master remote back on the coffee table. "That about does it." He pulled a thick sheaf of papers from his clipboard. "I just have some paperwork for you to fill out. Sign here."

Steven quickly scrawled his signature across

the bottom of the pages without reading any of them and handed the stack back.

The Cable Guy nodded and tucked the papers away in the chest pocket on his jumpsuit. "Thank you," he said. "That gave me power of attorney over you."

Steven stared at him. *"What?"*

"Joking," the Cable Guy said.

Oh. Good. Relieved, Steven laughed.

The Cable Guy joined him, but continued the laugh way too hard for way too long. When he finally stopped, there was an awkward silence. It was clear that, for some reason, the Cable Guy did not want to leave.

"Well. Guess I'm about finished here," the Cable Guy said finally, and then paused.

Steven nodded.

"Okay." The Cable Guy paused again, waiting for a response that didn't come. "Okay. I feel good about this." With that, he headed for the door.

Then it occurred to Steven that it was now or never. If he didn't at least *try* to get some premium channels free, Rick would never let him hear the end of it. Steven took a deep breath and trailed after the Cable Guy.

"Just one thing," he ventured.

The Cable Guy whirled around immediately, his eyes bright with anticipation. "Yeah!"

"I, uh, I have this friend," Steven said, without meeting his gaze, "and he said he gave his cable guy fifty bucks and he got free movie channels. Have you ever heard of anything like that?"

The Cable Guy stopped short, his expression deadly serious. "You mean, *illegal* cable?"

Steven bit his lip. This wasn't the reaction he had expected. "Uh . . . yes," he admitted.

"Who told you that?" the Cable Guy demanded. "I want his name!"

Okay. Big mistake. He shouldn't even have bothered trying. Steven held his hands up in complete denial. "Never mind. Forget it."

The Cable Guy dropped his toolbox on the floor and strode over, seemingly not ready to let it go at that. "You're offering me a bribe?" he accused Steven, standing only a few inches away from him. "I have to tell you that what you have just done is illegal, and in this state, if convicted, you could be fined five thousand dollars or spend six months in a correctional facility."

Oh wow, he was in *way* over his head now. "Please," Steven begged, trying not to panic as he saw his entire law-abiding life flash before his eyes. "That was dumb. I was just making conversation, I—"

The Cable Guy laughed suddenly. "I'm just kidding," he said, and reached out to tweak

one of Steven's ears. "Wake up, little snoozy!
I'll juice you up." He slung his arm around
Steven and walked him towards the front
door. "All it is, is the push of a button."

Steven let his breath out. *Good.* For a moment there, he'd been a little worried. "Oh
great," he said, reaching for his wallet. "How
much?"

"Don't worry about it," the Cable Guy said,
magnanimously waving the money aside. "I
*couldn't* charge you. I mean, your girl just
booted you. Consider it one guy doing another
guy a solid."

How about that? Maybe he'd misjudged this
guy. Steven shook his head admiringly. "That
is so nice. Thank you. You're sure I—"

The Cable Guy cut him off in mid-sentence.
"Hey, you're a nice guy. You'd be surprised
how many customers treat you like dirt, like
I'm just a plumber or something." He reached
into his pocket and then handed Steven a business card. "Here is my personal beeper number. It's just for my preferred customers. Never
call the company, they'll just put you on
hold."

Steven took the card and stuck it in his wallet. "Thanks. Really." Then he held up the
comment card. "You're gonna get some good
marks here."

The Cable Guy smiled shyly and dug one

shoe against the carpet. "Maybe some day, I'll take you out to the satellite, and show you how all this stuff works," he offered. "It's really incredible."

"Sure," Steven said with a vague shrug. "We should do that one day."

The Cable Guy's whole face lit up. "Okay! How 'bout tomorrow?"

What? Had he been *serious*? "Uh, tomorrow?" Steven repeated uncertainly. "Tomorrow's not good."

"What are you going to do?" the Cable Guy wanted to know. "Sit home and stew about your ex?"

Yes. "No," Steven said.

Now the Cable Guy looked very insulted. "Oh, okay. I guess I crossed the line." He flounced towards the door. "*Sorry*."

The poor guy seemed so upset that Steven couldn't help feeling kind of guilty. "No, you didn't cross the line," he lied.

The Cable Guy perked up again. "No? Cool! I'll pick you up at six-thirty." He headed for the door, and waved before he went out to the hall. "On the flip side!"

Then the door slammed, leaving Steven alone in his living room before he had time to reconsider his offer. He wasn't exactly sure how he had gotten roped into this, but apparently, he and the Cable Guy now had—a *date*?!

Weird.

*Too* weird.

The next morning, Steven got up extra early. He had a big presentation to give at work, and he wanted to be at his best. He did a hundred sit-ups, followed them with fifty push-ups, and even ate a noticeably well-balanced and nutritious breakfast. There would be no mid-morning slump for *him* today. He worked at a local real estate firm called Citywide Land Developers, and he was eager to move up the corporate ladder. *Yesterday*, if possible.

His presentation was scheduled for the weekly ten o'clock meeting, and all of the managers gathered around the shiny mahogany table in the main conference room. His boss, Hal Daniels, sat at the head of table, listening and nodding as Steven explained his latest idea.

This particular project was going to be a new condominium complex, and Steven was sure that it would be a fantastic development opportunity for the company, if they could just find the right investors. He had had this presentation in the works for weeks, complete with charts and graphs and other visual aids.

For his big finale, he whipped a sheet off an architect's model he'd had commissioned of the proposed complex.

"Here it is," he said confidently.

His coworkers leaned forward to survey the model, murmuring among themselves. The artist had done a great job, and the complex really looked snazzy.

"There are twenty-four classrooms, and each one can be converted into a 1,400-square-foot home," Steven told them, using a wooden dowel to point out various features on the model. "The facility has two tennis courts, an Olympic-size pool, and a full gym—with a stage, if the residents ever decide they want to perform *Oklahoma*."

Most of his coworkers laughed appreciatively. Years before, Steven had decided that if he was going to be a salesman, he was going to be a really good one.

"The kitsch appeal of living in an old schoolhouse should be very attractive to young, upwardly mobile home buyers," he went on, careful to use phrases that would sound enticing in the brochure. "And most important, the structure is available in foreclosure. If we put down a cash bid right away, we're going to steal this thing. I say we do it!"

There was a brief silence, and then everyone clapped. As the meeting broke up, Hal Daniels rushed over and put a proud arm around him.

"Yo, Steve-o!" Hal said enthusiastically.

"Tough room, but you got 'em. How are you doing?"

At the moment, he felt just wonderful. "Fine," Steven answered.

Hal reached up and self-consciously patted his hair, which had recently undergone the Sy Sperling treatment. "Okay. What?" he probed.

Steven shrugged his shoulders in complete innocence. "Nothing?"

"Yeah?" Hal said, but then looked at him more closely. "Did I hear something about you having a little domestic discord?"

The worst thing about working at a relatively small company was that it was almost impossible to keep any secrets. Steven thought he had been very discreet—but he was apparently mistaken. And with the way Hal was staring at him, he wasn't going to be able to avoid the issue.

"Robin and I have been having a difficult time," Steven conceded. "I moved out, but I really think it's only temporary."

"Gotcha," Hal said, and squeezed his shoulder unctuously. "I love this project, but it's a big one." He tilted his head to one side. "Can I be blunt? If I approve this and you mess it up, it's not going to be *my* responsibility. I have total confidence in you, but you hear where I'm coming from, right, Steve-o?"

Loud and clear. "Absolutely," Steven answered, making a point of sounding hearty. "Hey, look at it this way. Now that I'm on my own, I've got more free time than ever—it's a *good* thing."

"I can't look bad on this one," Hal said, and gave him a playful push. "But I know you're gonna do great."

"Thank you. I will," Steven promised.

Hal nodded and headed down the stairs to his office. Steven watched him disappear, and then turned to his secretary, Joan, who was typing furiously on her computer keyboard. "Hey, I'll be right back," he said.

Joan nodded without looking up, typing so swiftly that her fingers were a blur.

Steven felt like sharing his good news with someone, and there was only one person he wanted to tell. Unfortunately, she was also the one person who *really* didn't want to hear from him. Robin.

# Chapter Three

Robin Harris worked as a junior editor and features reporter at *Sassy* magazine, although in the last few months, she had advanced far enough up the career ladder to be given her own assistant. Mostly, though, she spent her time writing endless articles about dating, dieting, and teen heartthrobs. Sometimes she was able to combine all three within the same article.

Since he was afraid that she wouldn't take his call, Steven headed over to her office instead. If she saw him in person, maybe she would suddenly realize how much she missed him and beg him to come back. He had his pride, of course—but that didn't mean that he wouldn't do it in a second.

Steven strode through the halls at *Sassy*, smiling at a succession of young, confident, well-dressed women. For the most part, they managed to seem both chic and intellectual. Under any other circumstances, he might have taken his time and tried to chat a few of them up, but right now, he was a man with a mission.

Robin's office was just up ahead on the right, and he poked his head in her door. She was on the telephone, sounding brisk and businesslike as she took rapid notes on a legal pad. Her office was fairly nice, but it was clear that she wasn't at the upper level of the company yet. There were papers spread all over her desk, and the walls were covered with pictures from the magazine and various articles she had written.

Steven gave her a little wave and a *big* grin from the doorway. "Hello!"

Robin looked up from the telephone, and her face fell. She was in her late twenties and very attractive. She also had a very funky and unique sense of fashion that Steven didn't always quite understand but definitely admired. "I'll have to call you back," she said into the phone and then hung up. "Steven, what are you doing here?"

Unexpectedly nervous, he cleared his throat.

This was their first conversation since they agreed to spend time apart, and he didn't want to make things even worse.

"I was just in the area," he said, trying to seem casual. "Thought I'd pop by."

She just looked at him without speaking—or smiling.

Okay, so he'd already made the situation worse. "So, um—" He coughed. "I'm popping by."

She nodded, almost completely expressionless.

If he pretended everything was normal, maybe everything would *seem* normal. "How's work?" he asked brightly. "How'd the big teen crush article come out?"

"They liked it," she answered and then let out her breath. "I thought we agreed we weren't going to see each other for a month."

Well—yeah, he had kind of promised that he would respect her need for "space." Would she buy it if he said the agreement had just conveniently slipped his mind? Not likely. "I-I know, I know," he stammered uncomfortably. "It's just that Hal accepted my proposal to renovate the old schoolhouse, and I wanted to tell you right away."

"Oh. Well. That's wonderful, Steven," she answered, although her voice seemed more polite than enthusiastic. "Congratulations."

It wasn't quite the "Hooray! What great news!" he had been hoping for, but it would have to do. "I know I'm breaking the rules," he said, "but come have dinner with me tonight to celebrate?"

She sighed again and shook her head. "I really don't think we should."

Yeah, he had blown it, all right. Maybe he could still pull it out, though. He had always been good in the clutch. "Come on," he pleaded, with what he hoped was a winning smile. "This is the biggest day of my career."

It was quiet for a minute. When she finally spoke, her voice was very strained. "Please don't put me in this position, Steven," she said.

Okay, he would play dumb. Sometimes dumb worked. "What position?" he asked. "I'm not putting you in any position. Hal accepted my proposal, that's all."

She squirmed slightly in her chair and avoided his eyes, obviously feeling pressured. "Steven, I love you," she said, her voice overly patient, "but I need to take some time on my own to see how I feel. I mean . . . this is exactly why we broke up, because you never listen to me."

Hey, wait a minute! Wasn't she sort of rushing things here? "What?!" he protested. "Now we're broken up? What happened to 'trial separation?' "

Robin let out an irritated breath. "I'm sorry, I really can't get into this right now, Steven. If you haven't noticed, I'm at work."

Fine. Whatever. This was a lost cause. "Sorry to disturb you," he said stiffly, and turned to leave.

"Steven," she said after him, her voice softening. "Congratulations."

But he was still going to be celebrating alone, wasn't he? "Thanks," he said, and walked unhappily down the hall towards the exit.

So much for *that*.

That evening, when Steven got home from work, he changed out of his work clothes and took a shower. Then he sat down in his lonely living room to watch television. After seeing Robin, what should have been a great day had turned into a miserable one. He clicked the remote control from channel to channel in a daze, never stopping for more than a second.

At about six-thirty, a horn started honking outside.

"Steven!!" an unfamiliar voice bellowed. "Stev-ey!! Let's go! Yo, Steve!!!"

Steven got up from the couch as a very cheesy commercial for the "Medieval Times

Restaurant'' started playing. He walked over to the window and saw the Cable Guy standing in front of a white van, leaning in through the driver's side window to honk the horn.

The Cable Guy saw him and waved wildly. "Steven! Hey, buddy! Come on down! Shake a leg! Let's make hay while the sun shines! Be all that you can *be*, buddy!''

Steven waved back, and then stepped away from the window, not sure what to do. He didn't really feel like hanging out with his cable guy, but he didn't want to spend another evening alone either.

On the television, another commercial had just come on.

"Are you a smothering boyfriend who drives his girlfriend crazy?" the earnest announcer asked. "If so, call 55-JERRY.''

Steven looked back out the window and saw the Cable Guy smiling and waving for him to come down. He moved his jaw, and then began walking towards the front door.

"Oh, why not,'' he said.

How bad could a night with his cable guy be?

Steven walked outside to the customized van. The slogan THE CABLE COMPANY—GET WIRED TODAY was painted across the side.

"How's it going?'' he asked.

The Cable Guy nodded affably and opened

his door. "Howdy, partner. Climb aboard!"

Steven shrugged and got in on the other side.

The Cable Guy turned on the ignition and shifted the van into "Drive." He checked both ways, flicked on his signal indicator, and then pulled out into the street.

"Thanks for coming out," the Cable Guy said earnestly as he drove onto the main boulevard. "You know, most people think cable is just a simple co-ax that comes out of the wall. They never take the time to understand how it works."

Steven wasn't sure how to respond to that, but he smiled to be polite. "Uh, where exactly are we going?" he asked.

The Cable Guy's expression turned very grave. "We're going to take a ride on the information superhighway," he said in a deep voice. "Now. Do you think you're ready to hear the story of stories?"

Steven had the sudden sinking sensation that he was about to get a long riff about some evangelical religion. There was no question but that some proselytizing was in his immediate future. "I . . . guess so," he said uncertainly.

"Very well," the Cable Guy answered and closed his eyes briefly, even though he was still driving. "All right. It all started in Lansford, Pennsylvania, where Panther Valley Television, with the assistance of Jerrod Electronics, created the first cable television system.''

Steven nodded, smiled, and wished that he were someplace else—like with Robin, say. On the other hand, it was a nice night for a drive, and he didn't exactly have anything better to do. There were worse things than learning about the history of cable television.

''I visited Lansford once,'' the Cable Guy said, clearly awed by the memory. ''It's the Cable Guy's Mecca.'' He gulped noisily and paused to brush away a stray tear. ''It was very emotional.''

''Like Yonkers and Carvel,'' Steven said, just to make conversation.

''*Exactly*,'' the Cable Guy agreed. ''That is *so* deep, Steven.''

Steven shrugged sheepishly.

They drove up into the hills, steering up a long, winding road. Finally, the Cable Guy parked the van below a huge satellite dish. The dish was at the top of the small mountain, overlooking the entire city.

Twinkling lights spread out below them as Steven and the Cable Guy climbed out of the van. The place seemed pretty deserted, and Steven hung back dubiously, but the Cable Guy was already on his way down a thick-wooded trail. Steven ran to catch up.

"I come here to think sometimes," the Cable Guy volunteered. "To clear my head."

Steven nodded, then almost tripped over a large tree root. They turned a corner and ducked underneath some hanging vines. Now the satellite dish was right in front of them. It was *enormous*. A 150-foot radio antenna rose up above the dish, its tip disappearing into the dark night sky. Next to the antenna, there was a small fenced-in shack, where the dish controls were located.

"There she is," the Cable Guy said, proudly extending a hand in the dish's direction. "Right now, she's sending entertainment and information to *millions* of satisfied citizens."

"That's . . . pretty impressive," Steven answered.

The Cable Guy beamed at him. "See? I knew the moment I met you, that you would appreciate this."

Then the Cable Guy raced towards the satellite dish, with the same sort of excitement Maria had displayed while running down that hill in the Alps in *The Sound of Music*. A few seconds later, he appeared inside the dish with his arms raised.

"The future is now," he pronounced with great wonder. "Soon every American home will integrate their television, phone, and computer. TV will not be scheduled, it will all be on demand.''

Steven figured that this was probably the ''information superhighway'' part of the discussion.

''You'll be able to visit the Louvre on one channel and watch American Gladiators on another,'' the Cable Guy fantasized. ''You can do your shopping at home or play a game of Mortal Kombat with a friend in Vietnam. There's no end to the possibilities!'' He waved at Steven, who was still standing on the ground below the dish. ''Come on up! What are you waiting for?''

Standing in the middle of the satellite dish did actually look like fun, and Steven climbed up to join him. Soon they were both lying down, staring up at the stars. The view was fabulous, and it was very peaceful to lie there in the cool night air.

''Sometimes I'll sit here and imagine that there are billions of bits of information surging through me,'' the Cable Guy whispered.

Was that a comforting thought or a disturbing one? Either way, it was an *awesome* thought. ''I've watched a lot of TV in my life,'' Steven answered, ''but I guess I've always taken it for granted.''

It was quiet for a minute.

''When I was a kid, my mom worked

nights," the Cable Guy confided. "Never met Dad. But the old TV was always there for me."

Steven nodded, able to relate to that. "I know what you mean," he said. "My dad was there, but he might as well have been gone. My mom is a stewardess. She was always out of town."

"That's tough," the Cable Guy said sympathetically, and Steven could tell that he was moved by the confession. "You must have a lot of abandonment issues. Reality isn't *Father Knows Best*, it's a kick in the face on Saturday night with steel-tipped Kodiak boots and a trip to the hospital for reconstructive surgery. But what doesn't kill us makes us stronger, right?"

Steven started to speak, but then hesitated. Did they know each other well enough for him to bring this up? After all, it wasn't as though the guy didn't *know* what a terrible lisp he had. "Um, you know, my brother's a speech therapist," he said tentatively.

The Cable Guy sat up angrily. "So?"

Steven realized that he had gone too far, but he wasn't sure how to repair the damage, other than just changing the subject. "Never mind," he mumbled.

The Cable Guy lay back down, pretending that Steven had never mentioned it. They stared up at the stars in complete silence for a few minutes.

"So, you're pretty lovestruck about your lady, huh?" the Cable Guy said finally.

Steven could hardly deny that, so he just sighed. "I miss her," he admitted. "I asked her to marry me, and she asked me to move out."

The Cable Guy winced, empathizing with him. "I hate it when that happens."

Steven wasn't too thrilled about the situation himself. "She said she felt pressured." He shook his head. "Can you believe that?"

The Cable Guy thought that over, his lips pursed together reflectively. "Women are a labyrinth," he said finally. "Can I be frank? I don't think you listen to her."

Even if this was payback for bringing up the lisp, Steven didn't feel like hearing any criticism, so he folded his arms across his chest.

"I think you try to tell her what she wants to hear," the Cable Guy went on earnestly. "She wants you to thirst for knowledge about who she is. All the complicated splendor that is woman. When your loving is truly giving, it will come back to you tenfold."

Wow, this guy was genuinely, honestly *deep*. "You're right," Steven said, terribly impressed. "That is remarkably insightful."

"Yeah," the Cable Guy agreed. "It was Jerry Springer's final thought on Friday's show. He really knows how to sum it up."

Steven could think of no response to that whatsoever.

They stayed in the satellite dish for a long time. But it was getting pretty late, and they both had to go to work the next day, so finally they decided to head home.

"Time to hit the road, I guess," the Cable Guy said sadly.

Steven glanced at his watch and groaned. "Wow, is it ever."

They got back in the van, and the Cable Guy drove back to Steven's apartment building. He swerved to a stop right in front of the entrance, the brakes squealing.

Steven unsnapped his seat belt. "Well. This has been really—"

"You know what?" the Cable Guy burst out unexpectedly. "Women are suckers for *Sleepless in Seattle*. It's on HBO this month. That's your bait right there."

Actually, that sounded like a pretty good idea. "Robin loves that movie," Steven conceded.

"They all do," the Cable Guy said confidently. "Next time you talk to her, tell her you're cooking yourself dinner and watching it by yourself, and sound like you've never been happier. She'll come running. If it's one thing I know about, it's the effect of Tom Hanks on a female demographic. He is the embodiment of everything that is good and safe." Then he nodded once to punctuate that.

Well, it was worth a shot. Steven shrugged. "Maybe I'll give it a try." He started to get out of the van, then paused. "You know what? I'm embarrassed to say this, but I don't know your name. What is it?"

The Cable Guy's mouth dropped open. "You really want to know my name?" he gasped, clearly touched. "You do? Really? It's Ernie Douglas. But my friends call me Chip."

For some reason that rang a bell, but Steven wasn't sure why. "Well, okay," he said and reached for his door handle. "I'll see ya, Chip."

Before he could exit the van, the Cable Guy was staring deep into his eyes.

"Let's just remember right now," he said with such tremendous intensity that his voice shook. "You know, some people walk through their entire lives and never find a true friend." He paused significantly. "I guess we're the lucky ones."

Steven was a little taken aback, and he leaned away from him. "Uh . . . good-bye," he said lamely.

The Cable Guy grinned and flicked him a

quick goofy salute. "Later, buddy," he said happily. "I'll catch ya on the flip side!"

The abrupt change in the Cable Guy's mood was jarring, but Steven was relieved to get out of the van. The Cable Guy waved and beeped his horn repeatedly as he drove away. Steven waved back, feeling a little uncomfortable.

It had been a very bizarre evening.

# Chapter Four

Even though Steven suspected the Cable Guy—Cliff—whatever—might be more than slightly cracked, most of the romantic advice he had given made sense. Whatever he was doing right now with Robin wasn't working, and he was open to trying a new approach. He would do *anything* to get her back.

So the next day, as soon as he found a break in his schedule, he got her to meet him at a coffeehouse near the *Sassy* magazine building. Robin didn't exactly seem thrilled about the idea, but at least she showed up. He ordered her a double-decaf, nonfat latte, got a plain cappuccino for himself, and then indicated a table in the far corner. Reluctantly, she followed him across the coffeehouse, and they sat down.

Steven took a deep breath, ready to woo her with everything he had. "I don't listen to you," he said simply. If it worked for Jerry Springer and the Cable Guy, maybe it would work for him, too. "I *pretend* to understand, but I'm really just saying what I think you want to hear. So from now on, I'm going to try my best to listen more, because I *do* love you and am interested in learning about every detail about the complicated splendor that is you."

Robin just stared at him, shocked by what she was hearing. "Oh," she said, after a pause.

Oh? He had given a speech of great beauty and wisdom, and that was her *entire* reaction? Steven decided to try again. "I really want us to get back together, Robin," he said sincerely. "But I can see why taking this time apart might be good for us. So I'm not mad."

There was a short silence, and then a smile spread across Robin's face.

"Sometimes time apart is healthy," she said.

And sometimes, time apart was just depressing. "You're right," he agreed, nodding several times for emphasis. Hadn't the Cable Guy said something about leaving her wanting more? "Well, that's what I came here to say." He gulped down most of his cappuccino, and started to stand up. "Look, I've got to get back to the office."

She started to say something, bit her lip, and then went ahead and spoke. "So, you doing anything tomorrow?"

It worked! The Cable Guy—and Jerry Springer—were *geniuses*. He shrugged casually. "Oh, I don't know. I'm just going to cook myself dinner and watch a movie. *Sleepless in Seattle* is on cable."

Her eyes lit up. "Really?"

Yes, the Cable Guy unquestionably, if improbably, had his finger on the pulse of American womanhood. Steven finished his cappuccino and tossed the cup into a nearby trash can. "If you're around," he said, "you should drop by and check out the new apartment."

She hesitated for a second, but then nodded. "Okay. Maybe I will."

Yes! "Okay then," Steven responded and walked away, trying to hide his smile.

On the television in the corner of the coffee-house, a news update on the Sam Sweet trial was being shown on MTV, with Tabitha Soren anchoring the story.

"Today, in the Sam Sweet case, the prosecution played the 911 call that Sam Sweet made the night he murdered his brother," she was reading from a teleprompter. "Keep in mind he confessed one month later."

The camera cut to a shot of the courtroom and Sam Sweet sitting behind the defendant's table. Everyone was listening to the 911 call, and a transcription ran along the bottom of the screen.

"Hello, please send help," Sam Sweet was babbling on the tape between noisy, gulping sobs. "My twin brother has been shot!"

"Slow down, sir," a calm 911 operator responded. "What happened?"

"They shot him with a shotgun four times!" Sam Sweet screamed on the tape. It was easily the best performance of his entire career. "I mean, I think it was a shotgun. Who would do such a thing? I think it was an Asian gang or something. They were speaking some other language."

In the courtroom, Sam now leaned over and whispered something in his lawyer's ear. The lawyer nodded and made a quick note on his legal pad.

Now the camera cut back to Tabitha Soren in the MTV studio.

"Mmmm," she said ironically, not hiding her disapproval. "Who indeed?" Then she smiled. "That's the news for now. Coming up next, a rare interview with the First Lady."

Watching the end of the report before leaving the coffeehouse, Steven couldn't help laughing.

Only in America.

Every week, Steven played pickup basketball with a group of old friends, including his buddy Rick. They would meet at a local high school gymnasium and then go all-out for a couple of hours. It was always a competitive game but also a friendly one. The usual protocol was that if you knocked someone down, you had to smile when you helped him back up. Steven had known most of these guys for years, and he always looked forward to their games. It was a great way to blow off a lot of frustration and steam.

Today was their regular game day, and Steven's last meeting ran long so he almost didn't make it on time. The rest of the players were already shooting around by the time he made it over to the gym.

They chose up sides without much argument, then jumped right into a hard-driving game. Steven was on the skins team, while Rick was playing with the shirts.

Steven was so happy about the way his coffeehouse talk with Robin had gone that he played better than he had in weeks. Every time he touched the ball, it either went swishing through the net, or he threaded a perfect pass to one of his teammates through a pack of defenders. Today, despite being somewhat height-challenged, he was Shaq, Magic, and Michael all rolled up into one.

He got free from Rick, who was guarding him, yet again and threw his right arm up in the air. "Here, here, here!" he yelled. "I'm open!"

Instantly, one of his teammates whipped a swift pass in his direction. Steven neatly side-stepped Rick, snagged the pass one-handed, and drove to the basket. He eluded the other team's hulking center, flipped in an easy lay-up, and then punched his fist in the air in celebration.

Rick groaned, not sure how Steven had slipped away from him to score again. "My fault, my fault!"

"Not your fault," Steven assured him. "I'm in the zone. There's no stopping me today."

"You *wish*," Rick said.

"You *know*," Steven retorted, then they both laughed. The fact that it was a competitive game didn't mean that they couldn't still have fun.

Play resumed again. A player named Jeff took the ball out, and then passed to a heavy-set guy named Harry, who caught the ball and moved towards the basket. But before he made it into the key, he twisted his ankle and fell down. The ball squirted out of his hands and rolled toward the sidelines.

The ball rolled out of bounds and into a dark corner of the gymnasium. It hit a man's sneaker, and then a pair of hands reached down to pick it up. He was holding another ball under his arm, and he started dribbling both of them in a circular pattern. As the man straightened up, Steven saw, to his complete surprise, that it was . . . the Cable Guy.

"Hey, you guys play here too?" he chirped, then smiled broadly at Steven. "Weird. I mean, *cool*." He kept dribbling. "I was just out and about. Thought I'd see if anybody wanted to play some round ball."

Steven sighed. He hoped that this was just a coincidence, but somehow, he didn't think so.

Rick gestured towards Harry, who was still on the floor, gripping his ankle. "Great. We need another man."

Everyone was looking expectantly at Steven, who forced himself to smile.

"This is, uh, Chip Douglas," he said. "My cable guy."

Hearing the name, Rick smiled in recognition.

"We met about a week ago during a routine installation," the Cable Guy explained to the group in general, "but I feel like I've known him my whole life."

Steven shook his head, unable to believe that this was really happening. Were the movers and his new building superintendent and the exterminator going to start following him around all over the place too? Treating him like the brother none of them—with his luck—had ever had?

Everyone was exchanging glances, and Rick was the first one to break the silence, grinning broadly.

"Oh really. That's . . . sweet," he said, with sarcasm dripping from his voice. "All right, Chip Douglas, you're on shirts. Let's play."

The Cable Guy shook his head vehemently. "No, I want to be on Steven's team."

"Okay, fine," Jeff said with a shrug. "I'll switch teams. Let's just play."

"Okay, wait a sec, I've got to warm up," the Cable Guy said.

After stretching dramatically, he started running wind sprints back and forth across the court, touching all of the main lines in turn.

Everyone stared at him until he finished. Since this was just a social pickup game, none of them ever bothered doing anything as ambitious as wind sprints. For that matter, none of them ever even jogged in place. Usually they just did routine things like—tie their shoes.

"Let's get it on!" the Cable Guy yelled, his face bright red from his exertions.

"Are you any good?" Steven asked dubiously. There had been something very unconvincing about the display of energy and hustle.

The Cable Guy flashed him a cocky grin. "Feed me under the board, and you'll find out."

Play began, and Jeff moved to half-court to take the ball out.

"Let's see what you got, White Shadow," the Cable Guy said, moving to guard him.

Jeff shrugged, and started dribbling.

The Cable Guy was instantly all over him, covering him as tightly as humanly possible. He waved his hands in Jeff's face, whacked him in the back as he dribbled, and was generally as annoying as could be.

Jeff broke away from him for a second and passed the ball to Rick, who drove to the basket. He sent up a shot, which went in, and he and Jeff slapped hands.

"Traveling!" the Cable Guy screeched, making the referee's signal for the call by rolling his hands in a rapid circle. "That's traveling!"

Rick laughed, and ran past him towards the

other end of the court. "Yeah, right, whatever you say, *Chip*."

Everyone else kept playing too.

"All right, so we're playing *that* type of game," the Cable Guy said grimly. "Prison rules. *I* get it."

No one even glanced over at him as the game continued full-tilt. Steven's team passed the ball around, and the Cable Guy ran all over the court like a wild man, trying to get open. He crisscrossed back and forth, shouting and waving his arms. The guy covering him, Mike, tried to keep pace with him, but the Cable Guy was racing around as though his mother's life depended on it.

"Feed me the rock!" he screamed at the top of his lungs. "Feed me the rock! I'm open! I'm so open! I'm dyin' of loneliness here!"

A teammate passed the ball to Steven, and the Cable Guy came out of nowhere to grab it, so that he and Steven were fighting over possession.

"Come *on*, Steven," he said. "No man is an island."

"I'm on your team!" Steven protested.

The Cable Guy just ripped the ball out of his hands and drove towards the basket, shoving Jeff roughly out of the way in the process. The ball went in, and the Cable Guy made a sharp buzzing sound, along with the hand signal for a foul.

"And *one!*" the Cable Guy announced. "That's definitely a foul!" He stepped up to Jeff with a sneer, standing only inches from his face. "You want to mug me, my wallet is in my pants. I mean, my wallet is in my . . . you know what I mean."

Jeff looked disgusted and backed away from him.

Watching this spectacle—or, more accurately, *disaster*—Steven couldn't have been more embarrassed. It was bad enough to have the guy following him around, but it added insult to injury to have him show him up in front of everyone else like this.

"What are you doing?" he asked accusingly.

The Cable Guy frowned and shook a critical finger at him. "Come on now. Don't play from fear, Steven," he advised. "We can take these guys!"

Steven just rolled his eyes and kept playing.

As the game progressed, the Cable Guy's behavior got even worse and Steven felt as though he were watching the entire scene in vivid, slow-motion.

First, the shirts put up a shot, which didn't go in. The Cable Guy waded into the crowd around the basket, swinging his elbows wildly as he pulled down the rebound.

Then the Cable Guy drove toward the basket again, violently taking down two men, including Rick, and shrieking, "Foul, foul, foul! Not fair!" Once again, everyone just ignored him.

When play continued, Rick headed in for a shot. On his way, he faked Steven out. Off-balance, Steven fell down and watched Rick score from his position on the floor. The Cable Guy helped him up, glaring at Rick the entire time.

Walking back across the center line, he banged shoulders with Rick. Rick scowled at him but shook it off. Steven was taking the ball out, and the Cable Guy caught his in-bounds pass and brought the ball up the court.

"Don't worry," he muttered confidentially. "I've got his number."

Steven frowned, not sure what or who he meant by that.

At half-court, the Cable Guy fired a no-look bullet pass, nailing Rick right in the head. Rick was stunned by the blow, and the ball flew out of bounds.

"Sorry," the Cable Guy said flippantly. "I thought you were skins."

Rick just turned away from him, rubbing the spot above his ear where the ball had landed.

Steven's team in-bounded the ball at half-court, and when someone passed it to Steven, he drove for the basket. He missed the shot, his momentum carrying him out of bounds.

The Cable Guy stepped on Rick's back and leaped into the air, slam-dunking the rebound into the basket with two hands. He hung on the rim as the backboard shattered, raining glass all over the court.

Everyone else stood there in silence and stared at the wreckage.

"Well, I guess that's the game," a guy named Joel said with a disappointed sigh.

Everyone else nodded and slowly began filing off the court.

Steven closed his eyes, utterly mortified. The Cable Guy brought new dimensions to the concept of "unsportsmanlike conduct."

Jeff glared over at Steven. "Thanks for bringing your 'friend,'" he said sarcastically.

Steven sighed and rubbed his hand across his forehead, as he felt a terrible headache start between his eyes. He had been playing with these guys for years, and now they were never going to want to see him again. Rick in particular.

Feeling chipper, the Cable Guy bounded over to Rick to try and shake his hand.

"Good game," he congratulated him, and then gave Rick a congenial slap on the back. "You were tough out there. Your play brought me up to a higher level. I mean that."

"Yeah," Rick said dismissively, then turned his back on him.

Everyone except Steven left the gym right away, without speaking or looking back. As a rule, they all went out together after they played, but no one seemed to be in the mood anymore.

Steven scowled at the Cable Guy. "What's wrong with you? What were you *doing*?"

The Cable Guy shrugged guiltlessly. "It was payback time. I was protecting you."

Yeah, right. As though he *needed* protection from his best friend. "You ruined the game," Steven said and strode over to the sidelines to put his T-shirt back on.

The Cable Guy's eyes narrowed. "I don't appreciate your tone, Steven," he said softly. "That's not the way friends speak to each other."

"What are you talking about?" Steven snapped back at him. "I don't even know you!"

The Cable Guy grinned and slung his arm around Steven's shoulders. "Well, let's fix that. Let me buy you a drink," he said.

Steven shook his head and picked up his gym bag. "No, I'm going home."

"All right, then, well, uh, I guess we'll talk later," the Cable Guy said tentatively. "I've got to go shower up and do some stuff. I'll call you if I get a chance. Or you call me . . . or something."

He put his hand up for Steven to high-five, and Steven slapped it half-heartedly. Then the Cable Guy extended his palm out low by his knee.

"And down *low*," he said.

Steven stared at it without moving.

"Down low," the Cable Guy repeated, more than willing to wait there with his hand out for as long as it took.

It was obvious that he wasn't going to give up, and Steven finally tried to give him a low-five just so he could leave. Escape, actually. But the Cable Guy yanked his hand away at the very last second, so Steven missed it.

"Too slow," the Cable Guy said triumphantly. "Have a good one!"

"Yeah," Steven said under his breath as he walked away. "Have a good one."

At the moment, he was regretting ever having called the cable company and ordering service in the first place.

# Chapter Five

The next night was his possible date with Robin, and Steven was very excited. He knew he couldn't count on it, but if she stopped by, he wanted everything to be perfect. He had spent most of the afternoon shopping for just the right ingredients for cooking a gourmet meal. Just in case. He kept discovering that he was out of crucial ingredients and would have to run out to the grocery store to pick up fennel, or a jar of capers, or something similarly obscure.

He had just returned from his fourth emergency trip to the store; this time, to stock up on diet soda—a must, whenever Robin was around. He noticed that the light on his answering machine was blinking. And blinking, and blinking, and *blinking*.

When had he become so incredibly popular? Not that he didn't have friends, but considering how often he checked the machine, that many messages seemed a little excessive. Steven frowned and pressed the play button.

"You have eleven messages," the metallic automated voice on the machine announced.

*Eleven*? Steven pulled an onion from the grocery bag and started chopping it. If he threw together some homemade chutney, Robin would be really impressed.

There was the sound of rewinding, then a beep.

"Steve, it's Mom," his mother's voice said. "Give me a call. I'm still your mother . . ."

Then it was his father's turn to gripe at him.

"I'm getting on," his father's voice said, sounding very stern. "Steven, *call your mother*."

Steven winced. Okay, he wasn't as good about keeping in touch as he could be, and he knew that his mother spent a lot of time worrying about him. But he just hadn't felt up to telling his parents that he and Robin were not experiencing idyllic happiness lately, so he had been avoiding them. Even though they would promise not to take sides, they would be sure that it was all his fault, and no matter what he said, he wouldn't be able to convince them otherwise.

Especially since it was probably true.

There was a beep.

"Hey, Steven," the Cable Guy's voice said cheerily. "Just checking in. Give me a ring. I'm at 555-4329."

Naturally: the Cable Guy. Who else? Steven shuddered and kept chopping.

There was another beep.

"What's up, Steven?" the Cable Guy wanted to know. "I'm at a pay phone. If you're there, pick up." There was a pause. "Pick up. Pick up." Another long silence passed. "Okay, I'll be home later. I'll talk to you then."

Too needy for words. Steven shook his head and chopped his onion.

There was yet another beep.

"Okay, I'm home now," the Cable Guy's voice said, panting slightly. "Give me a buzz when you get in. I'll be here pretty much all night. Bye."

Beep.

"Hey, Steven!" the Cable Guy's voice boomed. "Quick question, give me a call when you get a chance."

Beep.

"I was out of the room for a minute," the Cable Guy's voice confided. "Thought you might have called. Okay. Later."

Beep.

"Sorry," the Cable Guy's voice said breathlessly. "I had call waiting, didn't get to it, thought it might have been you. All right, bye."

By now, Steven had given up on chopping his onion. Listening to this endless stream of frantic messages was beginning to freak him out a little. He started fast-forwarding through a sampling of the rest of the calls, discovering that every single one of them was from his pushy new friend that he didn't want.

"We're having ourselves quite a little game of phone tag here," the Cable Guy said at one point, sounding rather strident. "You're it!"

Steven fast-forwarded further along the tape.

". . . I was just blow-drying my hair and I thought I heard the phone . . ." the Cable Guy said, his voice getting increasingly shrill with each call.

This was really creepy. Steven fast-forwarded.

". . . you're a tough man to reach," the Cable Guy said ominously.

Steven fast-forwarded again, and this time, the Cable Guy sounded pitiful.

". . . I guess you're too busy to call your friends," he was saying.

Steven fast-forwarded to the final message,

and heard a long silence, followed by sighing.

"Where are you?" the Cable Guy asked quietly and hung up.

Steven stared uneasily at his answering machine. Implausible as it seemed, he felt almost as though he was being stalked or something. Maybe he should try getting an unlisted phone number. Just then, the doorbell rang, and he jumped about a foot off the floor.

He took a deep breath to pull himself together, then went over to open the door.

It was Robin, although he was still too shook-up to really appreciate the enormity of her coming over like this. She was dressed casually in leggings, an oversized sweatshirt, and aerobic sneakers, but she still looked beautiful.

Then again, as far as he was concerned, she *always* looked beautiful.

Robin smiled at him apprehensively. "Uh, hi. Uh, is everything all right?"

Yeah, he had probably looked pretty wild-eyed when he first opened the door. "Everything's fine," he answered. "Hey, it's good to see you."

She nodded a couple of times, looking everywhere but at him. "Uh, yeah. You too."

There was an awkward moment as Steven intentionally didn't kiss her hello. Tonight was the low-pressure selling technique all the way.

"Well," she said and looked uncomfortable once she realized that he wasn't going to kiss her.

Steven moved away from the door and gestured for her to come inside. "Come on in," he said. "What do you think of the place?"

Robin walked into the apartment and gazed around the room curiously. The furniture in the living room was still grouped in front of the television set, exactly the way the Cable Guy had left it.

"You made some interesting choices laying out the room," she remarked.

Steven flushed and ran a self-conscious hand back through his hair. "That's actually where the movers put the furniture," he improvised off the top of his head. "I'm going to change it, very soon."

"No," she assured him. "I like it. Really."

"Oh," Steven said. Did she mean that or was she just being polite? To play it safe, he decided to take her at her word. "Well . . . it's been growing on me."

His culinary efforts were a reasonable success, but their attempts at having a normal conversation were a disaster. After they finished eating, they sat awkwardly together in the living room.

"So," Robin said finally, after a lengthy silence. "How's work?"

Steven nodded. "Work's good. Yeah."

It was quiet again.

"How's Hal?" she asked.

Well, at least he had *plenty* of opinions when it came to his boss. Steven shook his head. "Don't get me started," he said, feeling animated for the first time all night. "That guy has no vision. It's like working for Mr. Magoo. And those hair plugs. Does he think nobody notices?"

"It's just great that he approved your project," Robin said. "It's a real step up."

"I know," Steven agreed. "Now, if only someone at Corporate would smarten up enough to dump *Hal*, I could really get some stuff done."

Robin nodded, then there was another lull in the conversation.

"It's, um, nice to see you doing so well," Robin said, to break the silence.

He might as well try to escalate this a little. "Well, it's nice just to see *you*," Steven told her.

Robin looked slightly uncomfortable. "Yeah."

More silence.

"Well." Steven glanced at his watch. "Hey, it should be starting."

They got up from the table in the dining alcove to go sit on the couch instead. Steven turned off the stereo with one remote and picked up another to activate the television. He turned it on, and to his dismay, the screen was filled with white noise and static.

"Oh no. The cable is out," he said, gritting his teeth. Of all times for this to happen, with *Sleepless in Seattle* starting any minute now. He got up and went to check the connecting wires on the back of the television.

"It's all right," Robin said. "We can watch it another time."

"No, no," Steven insisted. "We really should see it now. Now's a good time." He played with the remotes, hoping that the reception would come back magically, but no matter which remote he tried, it didn't.

"It's really all right—" Robin started.

Steven shook his head. "No, it isn't. It isn't right at all." Then he thought of the only possible solution. He didn't want to do it, but the stakes here were very high. "Wait, wait. I know what to do."

He ran to the kitchen and grabbed the Cable Guy's beeper number.

"The Cable Guy's a friend of mine," he told Robin confidently. "I'm a preferred customer. I'll just page him. We'll have this fixed in no time." Quickly, he dialed the Cable Guy's beeper, and punched his phone number in. "I hate pagers," he admitted, as he listened to the various mechanical sounds on the other end.

Just as he hung up, there was a sharp rap on the door. Steven looked surprised, and walked across the room to open it.

The Cable Guy was standing there, looking dark and disturbed. It was as though his personality had changed completely, and Steven was startled by the animosity in his expression.

"That was ... fast," he said weakly.

The Cable Guy showed all of his teeth in a tight smile. "Is there a problem with your service?" he asked, with even his lisp sounding hostile.

"Yeah," Steven answered. "My cable went out."

Then he pushed the Cable Guy out into the hall and closed the door partway behind them. The last thing he wanted was to get Robin involved—in any way—with this guy.

"Really?" the Cable Guy asked, and then he held up a cut cable cord. "And so you called me." He paused, tapping the cable cord rather menacingly against his palm. "Interesting how you call when you *need* something. Is that how you treat people?"

Okay, so this was revenge for the eleven unanswered messages on his machine. Steven sighed. "I've just been really busy. Look, you've got to get my cable going, Robin is here. This is *really* important."

The Cable Guy nodded and peeked into his apartment to get a look at Robin. The two of them made momentary eye contact before Steven dragged him back out to the hall again, shutting the door behind them.

"I see," the Cable Guy said, with his lips pursed. "Robin is important. But calling me back isn't?"

Feeling a truly terrible headache coming on, Steven rubbed his temples. "I'm sorry, okay?" he apologized. "Please, you've got to help me."

The Cable Guy considered that. "Why should I help you?" he mused. "I gave you free cable. What have you ever done for me?"

Talk about being put between a rock and a hard place. "Anything you want," Steven promised frantically, hoping that Robin wouldn't get impatient and decide to leave. "Name it—*quickly*."

"Okay," the Cable Guy agreed. "Tomorrow night, we hang out."

With the success of his date being held hostage to his cable reception, Steven was in no position to argue. "Fine," he said. "Whatever you want."

The Cable Guy looked visibly moved by that. "You're too good to me." He went over to a fuse-type box in the hall, turned one knob, and walked back to Steven. "All set!"

Steven frowned at him suspiciously. That was it? "So, what's with the cut cord?" he asked.

"That's for effect," the Cable Guy answered nonchalantly. "See ya tomorrow, Steven." Then he leaned closer, with a conspiratorial note in his voice. "She's pretty."

Steven nodded, impatient to get back inside.

"And don't kiss her," the Cable Guy said, sounding very sure of himself. "Fight the urge at all costs. It'll pay off later. Enjoy the flick," he added, and headed down the hall.

Shaking his head, Steven walked inside his apartment and shut the door. The guy was a lunatic.

"Who was that?" Robin asked from the couch.

"Nobody," Steven answered, and sat next to her on the couch.

The television was working perfectly now, and he flipped to the channel showing *Sleepless in Seattle.* Robin leaned against him, and Steven put his arm around her. They began to cuddle together as the movie started.

Even if the price for this happiness was another evening hanging out with the Cable Guy, it was more than worth it . . .

\*   \*   \*

After leaving Steven's building, the Cable Guy sat alone in the back of his van and watched *Sleepless in Seattle* on a small television. Except for the flickering light coming from the television set, it was very dark, but the Cable Guy felt right at home. Of course, that was only natural, since he lived in his van.

As he sat there, alone in the darkness, he suddenly remembered being a child and spending his days and nights watching television all by himself. The only happy childhood memories he had revolved around the joy he got from watching television. He stared into space, hearing a haunting version of the television theme to *My Three Sons* in his mind. *My Three Sons* was his favorite show of all time.

He remembered living in a dismal, cheap apartment with his mother, back when he was eight years old. The place was always filthy, with empty take-out food containers lying all over the floor. The only furniture in the living room was a ratty old plaid couch that smelled like cigarette smoke, and a black-and-white television.

That particular night, he was watching *My Three Sons*. The Douglas brothers were, as always, having fun, and he had wished more than anything that he could be one of them.

As he watched the show with his mouth

hanging open, his mother came stumbling into the room, looking tired.

She was forty years old and always wore cheap clothes and too much makeup. "Okay, Mommy's going out," she said.

He remembered looking up at her sadly and wondering why she never stayed home or spent any time with him. "When am I going to get a brother?" he asked. "You said I was getting a brother to play with."

"First Mommy's got to find a man," she answered, her voice bitter. "Now you watch your friend, Mr. Television. He'll take care of you."

He nodded obediently.

"And don't sit too close," she said, as she left. "You'll rot your brain out."

Then the front door slammed, and he was alone. He got up and moved closer to the television. The closer he got, the safer he felt. This was years before remote controls had been invented, and he rested his hand on the channel dial so that he could change the channel whenever he wanted. He stared at the television in a trance, periodically changing channels.

Even now, years later, sitting by himself in his dark van, watching *Sleepless in Seattle*, the Cable Guy still felt like that lonely little boy.

# Chapter Six

The next evening, the Cable Guy arrived at Steven's house fifteen minutes early and beeped the horn until Steven finally came outside. Steven had been trying to think of a good excuse to cancel their evening together, but so far he hadn't come up with anything more convincing than claiming that he "had a touch of the flu." Besides, maybe it would just be better to get this over with, and then the guy might leave him alone.

"Where are we going?" Steven asked, after he had gotten into the van and they exchanged brief hellos.

The Cable Guy smiled mysteriously. "That's for me to know . . ." he started.

". . . And me to find out," Steven finished dryly. Hadn't that particular retort gone out of fashion sometime back when he was in the third grade?

"Right!" the Cable Guy said.

They drove for a few miles, and then the Cable Guy pulled into a large parking lot. Before they got out of the van, he once again insisted that their destination was a secret and that Steven had to keep his eyes closed until he was told to open them.

Steven, reluctantly, cooperated. Not that he wasn't spontaneous, but frankly, he just *hated* being surprised.

"Sorry about yesterday," the Cable Guy said as he took Steven's arm and led him across the parking lot. "I was in kind of a weird mood. How'd things go? Keep 'em closed," he added, as an afterthought.

"Pretty well," Steven said. At least, he thought so. With luck, Robin agreed with that assessment. "We'll see." He started to open his eyes. "Look, about the other night. I didn't appreciate you—"

"Don't peek!" the Cable Guy ordered him. "I want this to be a surprise."

Steven still wasn't in the mood for any games, but he kept his eyes shut. "I really don't need to be surprised. Where are we going?"

"Only the best restaurant in town," the Cable Guy promised him, and then guided him around a sharp corner. "Okay, here we are," he announced. "Open sesame!"

Steven opened his eyes and saw an enormous faux castle with a large, tacky sign that read "MEDIEVAL TIMES RESTAURANT." *This* was the best restaurant in town? "Medieval Times?" he said doubtfully.

The Cable Guy nodded. "Yeah, I know what you're thinking. Don't worry, it's my treat."

That hadn't been even remotely what Steven was thinking, but he didn't argue.

Once they got inside, they were directed to a table overlooking a large, circular arena, which made it seem almost as though they were at a rodeo. The entire restaurant was designed in medieval-themed decor, and the staff members were dressed as knights, sorcerers, members of the royal court, and other medieval citizens.

"Funny," Steven said ironically. "I never thought I would actually come here."

"I love this place," the Cable Guy gushed. "I come here like twice a week."

From what Steven had seen so far, once in a *lifetime* was going to be enough for him.

Their waitress came slouching over to them, dressed in period clothes and looking very grouchy about the whole thing.

"Welcome to Medieval Times," she said flatly, without making eye contact with either of them. "My name is Melinda. I'll be your serving wench. May I get you something from the barkeep?"

The Cable Guy gestured for Steven to watch him in action. "Does thust have thou a hearty mug for me and me mate?" he asked much too enthusiastically. "He has been pitched in battle for a fortnight and has a king's thirst for the drink thust thou might have for thust."

The waitress didn't bat an eye. "I'll be right back, my lord," she said without much interest. Then she slogged off to the bar.

The Cable Guy swiftly assembled an object that was lying next to his plate. "There you go!" he said, handing Steven a paper crown.

Steven sighed, but they both put their crowns on.

"Look, this is kind of difficult to bring up," Steven began awkwardly.

Just then, trumpets sounded at the front of the room and the lights were lowered. The show—whatever it was—was about to begin.

"Hold that thought," the Cable Guy told him, his eyes dancing with excitement. "Show's on."

Steven rolled his eyes, but turned his chair so that he would be able to see.

A man who looked like a low-rent Alan Rickman from the movie *Robin Hood* started speaking to the crowd from the stage at the end of the arena.

"Welcome to a magnificent journey into the past," he said with a flourish. "*This* is Medieval Times!"

The crowd—most of whom were clearly tourists, deeply deluded ones, at that—applauded.

"All right! Are you prepared for a night of feasting and sport the likes of which you will never forget?" the host shouted.

The audience clapped harder.

"I charge you to stand up and cheer for your section's knight!" the host commanded.

Now Steven noticed that each section of the restaurant was painted a color that corresponded with a knight. The Cable Guy had already leaped to his feet and was cheering as though he was at a wrestling match.

Steven stayed right where he was, with his head lowered, praying that no one he knew would ever find out that he had come to this place.

"Let the games begin!" the Cable Guy yelled. "The Blue Knight rules! The Red Knight stinks! You're going down! Going *down*!"

Steven was acutely embarrassed, but he

tapped his hands together a couple of times to be polite.

So far, he was not having a fabulous time.

The show went on, and on, and on. Steven and the Cable Guy watched as two knights in the center of the room fought with swords while on horseback. They had ordered whole chickens, which they were apparently supposed to eat with their bare hands.

Their waitress, Melinda, hustled by them with a heavy tray of meals balanced on one shoulder, and Steven reached out to stop her.

"Excuse me, Melinda. Could I get a knife and fork?" he asked pleasantly.

She shook her head. "There were no utensils in medieval times, so there are no utensils *at* Medieval Times." She pushed a stray wisp of hair away from her face with the back of her hand. "Do you want a refill on that Pepsi?"

Oh, this was just too idiotic for words. "There were no utensils," Steven repeated, "but there was *Pepsi*?"

The waitress let out an exasperated breath. "Look, I have a lot of tables to get to," she said, and continued on her hurrying way.

Steven looked down at his chicken, shrugged, and ripped off a drumstick.

"So," the Cable Guy said with his mouth full. Eating with his hands clearly didn't faze him a bit. "What were you saying before?"

Before? Oh right, the conversation he had tried to start while they were walking into the restaurant. Well, he might as well try and get it out of the way once and for all. "How do I put this?" Steven asked rhetorically. "I've really enjoyed hanging out with you, but—"

The Cable Guy nodded and cut him off. "That's why I became a cable guy," he said happily. "To make friends like you. Every time I walk up to a new door, that door is a possibility for friendship. When I walked in your apartment, I knew there was something there." He beamed at Steven. "I just *knew* it."

"Oh man," Steven muttered under his breath. Then he tried to get the conversation back on track. "Look. I want you to know—"

"Can I have your skin?" the Cable Guy asked, indicating Steven's chicken. Then he took the skins from both of their chickens and put them on his face. "Look, *Silence of the Lambs*!" He lowered his voice to sound like an ominous Hannibal Lecter. "Hello, Clarice. . . ."

Steven closed his eyes. So much for what was left of his appetite.

The restaurant's lighting suddenly changed again, and trumpets played a loud fanfare as the host walked out onto the stage.

"We have reached the climax of our competition, good people!" he said portentously.

"Now, two noble men from our audience will battle to the death to resolve a grievance. Will a Master—" He stopped and glanced down at his clipboard—"Steven M. Kovacs and Lord Ernie Douglas make your way to the fighting pit!"

A bright spotlight shined on them, but Steven just stared at the host in shock.

The Cable Guy was already standing up. "Come on," he said. "Let's go."

Now Steven focused his gaze on the Cable Guy. "What's going on?" he asked.

The Cable Guy shrugged, taking one last gulp from his jumbo-sized mug of Pepsi. "It appears we're going to do battle, Steven."

This was a nightmare. Steven looked around and saw that all of the customers sitting nearby were also urging him to get up from the table. "Is, um, this a normal part of the show?" he asked.

The Cable Guy shook his head. "No, but I give all the knights free cable. They said it would be cool if we just went at it for a little while."

Steven started to protest, but two pimply-faced serfs from the show had come over to lead them away.

"Is this safe?" he asked uneasily.

The Cable Guy shrugged again. "That's what the armor's for."

Somehow, that didn't sound very safe.

At all.

The serfs guided them out to the center of the arena and helped them put on their armor. The Cable Guy had a huge grin on his face and was obviously enjoying every second of this, but Steven was freaked out by the whole scene. This whole thing seemed like a *really* bad idea.

"What are we supposed to do?" he asked, moving his armor-encased arms tentatively. The suit was even heavier than he might have guessed. "We've got to be careful we don't hurt each other, right?"

The Cable Guy, who already had his game face on, didn't answer him.

"Hey, look—" Steven began.

The Cable Guy interrupted him. "I cannot listen to any of your instructions, for you are my sworn enemy, and are about to meet your demise," he said.

Was he kidding or what? Before Steven could respond to that, the trumpets blared.

"Let the battle begin!" the host proclaimed. "Come now, people. Let me hear your voices!"

The crowd cheered, and stirring martial music reverberated from the huge speakers mounted on either side of the stage. The serfs handed Steven and the Cable Guy swords and shields before scurrying away to safety.

Instantly, the Cable Guy crouched down in a warlike position and began to circle Steven like a cat. Not sure what else to do, Steven mirrored his actions.

"Just take it easy," he warned.

The Cable Guy's response was to let out a piercing whoop and run towards him, swinging his sword wildly. Steven ducked down in terror, holding his shield up to protect his head. The Cable Guy slammed his sword down on the shield, and sparks flew everywhere.

"Oh no!" Steven said, trying to get out of the way as the Cable Guy lunged towards him again.

Clearly out for blood, the Cable Guy slashed at him with the sword. Steven leaped back, feeling a definite breeze as the sword whipped past him, only an inch or two from his face. Before the Cable Guy had time to try again, Steven ran about ten feet away, his armor clanking with every step.

"What are you doing?!" he shouted at the Cable Guy, completely enraged by all of this.

The Cable Guy shrugged. "I'm trying to kill you," he said in a matter-of-fact voice.

No kidding! Steven was going to yell at him some more, but the Cable Guy was already attacking him again. With a skill born of total panic, Steven blocked the sword with his shield and pushed him off.

"Nice move," the Cable Guy observed. "Necessity is the mother of invention."

Steven was having so much trouble catching his breath that he didn't bother trying to respond.

The Cable Guy turned and tossed his sword and shield over to the closest serf.

"Is it over?" Steven panted, more relieved than he could ever remember being.

The serf threw the Cable Guy a deadly looking mace. The Cable Guy caught the new weapon with one hand and then started chasing Steven around the fighting pit with it, screaming unintelligible threats.

Steven ran as fast as he could, his movements awkward in the cumbersome suit of armor. This entire scene was sheer insanity. He also couldn't help wondering what sort of insurance premiums Medieval Times had to pay. People could get seriously hurt in this place!

"Come back here!" the Cable Guy shouted across the arena, as he swung the mace back and forth, wielding it like a lethal baseball bat. "Right now!"

Steven was too busy trying to survive this fierce—and demented—struggle to answer him.

All of a sudden, the Cable Guy stopped short and grabbed his leg as though it had cramped up. "Oh, my leg," he moaned. "It's cramped."

Concerned that he might be injured, Steven walked over to see how he was.

"Are you all right?" he asked, worried.

"I am now!" the Cable Guy shouted and whirled around to whack Steven right in the head with his mace.

Steven flew backwards from the force of the blow, his helmet now obscuring his vision. His ears were ringing, and he shook his head a few times to clear them.

Then he reached up to fix his helmet, twisting it around to the right position—just in time to see the Cable Guy sprinting straight at him with the mace held high above his head.

If Steven had had enough time to think, his entire life would have been flashing before his eyes right now.

# Chapter Seven

The Cable Guy swung the mace at him, and reacting instinctively, Steven managed to block it with his shield. For the first time, he was suddenly furious and he rolled to his feet to fight back. If this was going to be a real fight, Steven had every intention of *winning*.

Using his sword with the deftness of a surgeon, Steven wrapped the chain of the mace around his blade. With one swift move, he jerked the mace out of the Cable Guy's hand and sent it flying across the arena.

The Cable Guy looked down at his empty hand, startled. "Whoa," he said, as he watched his mace land about twenty feet away.

While he was distracted, Steven butted him

with his shield as hard as he could, and the Cable Guy crashed down onto the dirt floor of the fighting pit in a heap of armor and tangled limbs.

"Whoa," the Cable Guy said again, then blinked. "*Ouch.*"

So angry that he was literally seeing red, Steven flung his sword and shield aside, and rushed towards the Cable Guy, fully prepared to kill him with his bare hands.

At the last possible second, the Cable Guy reached up and flipped Steven over onto his back in the dirt.

"That's the spirit," he said happily. "Let's give 'em a good show!"

Oh, so now this was just a *performance*? From upside down, Steven could see the Cable Guy crawling towards him, ready to attack. He quickly grabbed a handful of mud and threw it right into the Cable Guy's face.

"I'm blinded!" the Cable Guy groaned over-dramatically, grabbing his face with both hands. "Oh, my eyes!" He wiped the grit from them and glared at Steven. "So that's how it's gonna be, huh?"

Steven nodded and scrambled back to his feet, keeping his weight low and well-balanced so that he would be able to fend off the next assault.

"All right," the Cable Guy said, with a slow,

somewhat deranged, smile. "If you want to play rough, Daddy can play rough."

The ever-helpful serfs tossed them huge battle axes now to help escalate the fight. The axes were four feet long, with thick wooden handles and shining silver blades at the end of them. They were heavy, they were unwieldy, and they were *lethal*.

Steven and the Cable Guy began circling each other, each one hanging onto his ax with a death grip.

"This is just like when Spock had to fight Kirk on *Star Trek*," the Cable Guy observed merrily. "Best friends, forced to do battle."

Best *enemies*, as far as Steven was concerned.

As they leapt forward and crossed battle axes, the Cable Guy began to hum the *Star Trek* battle music. Gripping the blunt end of his ax, the Cable Guy swung the blade viciously at Steven and cut his shirt open.

Steven looked down in dismay. He liked this shirt. He didn't seem to be bleeding, but that one had been too close for comfort.

"Chip, this isn't funny!" he protested. "Will you stop it?!"

"The name is Spock," the Cable Guy responded mechanically, mimicking Spock's affectless voice. "If we don't battle to the death, they'll kill us both."

This was only supposed to be a little enter-

tainment for the crowd after their $9.95-all-
you-can-eat-complete-with-salad-bar dinners,
wasn't it? "This *isn't Star Trek*," Steven said
patiently.

The Cable Guy just looked at him without
blinking. "Good-bye, Jim," he said solemnly.

With that, the Cable Guy went into an elab-
orate, yet clumsy, martial arts-type move, using the battle ax as a prop. Steven just stared
at him, somewhere between amusement and
consternation.

The Cable Guy swung the ax around violently and held both ends to jump over and
then behind him. The move finally culminated
in a slow-motion roundhouse sweep which
upended Steven and put him flat on his back.

The Cable Guy stood up, holding his arms
in the air like a victorious warrior. Then he
marched towards the end of the arena where
the horses' entrance was.

Steven sat up, thankful that the fight was
finally over and he was still in one piece. The
whole incident had been pretty stressful, and
after having eaten that huge meal beforehand,
the truth was that he could really use a couple
of antacids right around now.

Failing that, maybe their sulky waitress
would bring him a ginger ale.

"Good fight," the show's host told him.

"Eat, drink, and be merry—and tip your waitress."

Then they both heard the sound of pounding horse hooves. Steven looked up to see the Cable Guy riding out to the arena, holding a jousting stick.

The show's host jumped up. "Quickly, muster atop your steed!" he said urgently.

Yeah, right. The people at this restaurant just didn't know when to quit. Steven shook his head and stayed right where he was.

Now the host dropped out of character. "Get on the horse!" he shouted frantically. "I don't think he's kidding!"

What?! Left with no choice, Steven jumped on the horse one of the serfs had brought out to the ring and grabbed a jousting stick from another frightened-looking serf.

This was a terribly tragic accident waiting to happen. "Don't do this!" Steven pleaded with him.

"I have no choice!" the Cable Guy yelled back. "Jim, my blood is boiling."

"I don't believe this," Steven said, and bent down in the saddle, pointing the jousting stick so that he would be able to defend himself. "Whoa!"

The show's host smacked Steven's horse, sending it straight toward the charging Cable Guy, and Steven hung on for dear life.

"Good luck, idiot," the host said after him, shaking his head.

They raced towards each other in a horribly dangerous game of chicken. If they were really going to do this, Steven had no intention of giving in—and he could tell that the Cable Guy wasn't going to, either.

When they reached one another, their horses galloping at top speed, Steven made the first move and knocked the Cable Guy off his horse with his jousting stick.

Struck right in the chest by the blow, the Cable Guy sailed through the air and landed flat on his back in the middle of the arena. There was a heavy thud when he crashed to the ground, and then he lay very still.

Shocked by what he had done, Steven turned his horse around and rode over to him. He yanked on the reins, pulling his horse to a quick stop. Then he jumped off, throwing away his helmet at the same time.

"Are you okay?" he asked anxiously.

The Cable Guy sat up and smiled at him, none the worse for the wear. "Well done, good sir," he said. "You are the victor, but we shall meet again."

Steven stared at him, stunned.

The two serfs lifted Steven up onto a wooden chair connected to two poles and hoisted him off the ground. They carried him to the center of the arena in a victory parade as all of the customers in the restaurant gave him a standing ovation.

Caught up in the adrenaline rush, Steven found himself grinning. He raised his arms in triumph, and the crowd cheered even more wildly.

For a ruthless fight to the finish, in a terribly tacky restaurant, the truth was that, in retrospect, it had actually been a lot of fun.

When they finally left Medieval Times, well-sated by several more rounds of Pepsi and lots of congratulations, Steven was still feeling the flush of victory. Not ready to call it a night yet, he invited the Cable Guy back to his apartment to hang out for a while.

"You've got a real warrior's instinct," the Cable Guy observed admiringly as they walked up the stairs to his apartment.

Steven nodded, still smiling. In fact, he had been grinning so hard, for so long, that his face was starting to hurt.

"I've got to admit, there's a real feeling of power holding that jousting stick," he conceded, feeling so energetic that he took the steps in a series of swift bounds.

"One thing's for sure, if Robin saw you tonight, she would be *begging* you to take her back," the Cable Guy said, keeping up with him effortlessly. "I'm telling you, these knights are what women love."

The life of a knight was much more exciting than being a real estate developer. "We should go again next week," Steven said eagerly.

The Cable Guy laughed and reached over to pat him on the head, the same way a person might pat a rambunctious puppy. "Easy there, Lancelot."

He didn't feel like Lancelot; he felt like the king! Steven unlocked his front door and motioned for the Cable Guy to follow him inside. He headed straight for the kitchen and hit a button on his answering machine.

"You have zero messages," the machine told him in its electronic voice.

"Nobody loves ya," the Cable Guy chuckled.

After being cheered for twenty minutes by a huge crowd, it was hard to get upset about not having any messages, so Steven just shrugged.

The Cable Guy opened the refrigerator, studied the contents, and helped himself to an orange soda. "Hey, I think I left something in the living room the other day," he said as he twisted the cap off with one quick move of his wrist. "Could you be a pal?"

Steven walked agreeably towards the living

room and flicked on the lights. Then he stared at the transformation that had taken place in his absence.

"What do you think?" the Cable Guy asked, sounding very pleased with himself.

Steven's entire stereo system and the twenty-seven-inch television had been replaced with a sixty-five-inch television, laser disc player, karaoke machine, and a brand-new, top-of-the-line stereo.

"What is this?" Steven asked, stunned by the array of gadgets.

The Cable Guy shrugged casually, although his eyes were bright with excitement. "It appears as if someone took the liberty of updating your in-home entertainment system," he said. "I got you the big-screen TV, deluxe karaoke machine, plus THX-quality sound that would make George Lucas a very happy camper."

Steven stared at all of the new electronics equipment. This was the entertainment system of his dreams, but he would never have been able to afford a setup like this. Then something occurred to him and he turned to look at the beaming Cable Guy.

"So wait. You went in my house when I wasn't home?" he asked.

The Cable Guy lifted his shoulders in a shrug. "How else was I supposed to get the stuff in here?" he pointed out logically. "Osmosis?"

Steven wasn't sure if he liked the idea of the guy just inviting himself in that way, but he walked over to examine the system more closely. "So wait. How much did this cost?" he asked as he bent down to look at the high-tech, multidisc CD player.

"Practically nothing," the Cable Guy assured him. "I have a connection. Preferred customer. I hook him up, he hooks me up."

Even so. He wouldn't even expect his best friend Rick to do something like this. For that matter, even his *parents*—who undeniably loved him a great deal, whenever they weren't disappointed in him—wouldn't buy him a setup this fancy. "Look, I can't accept this," Steven declared. "I wouldn't feel right."

The Cable Guy sat down on the couch and made himself at home. "Yes," he said, "but you give me something so much more valuable . . . *friendship*."

Oh boy. "And you've given me friendship too, so we're even," Steven answered. "Really, don't take it personally, but you've got to take it back."

The Cable Guy looked terribly disappointed. Crushed, even. "Well, okay, but my buddy with the pickup truck works all week," he said sadly. "Is it all right if I leave it here 'til Saturday?"

"Sure, no problem," Steven said, feeling guilty for having hurt his feelings. The poor guy had just been trying to do something nice for him—even if it was way beyond the call of duty. "And don't get me wrong, I really appreciate the gesture."

"Mm-hmm, mm-hmm," the Cable Guy answered, his voice distant. "It's cool." He got up from the couch, set his unfinished soda down on the coffee table, and walked over to the front door with his shoulders slumped.

As the door closed softly behind him, Steven sighed. No matter what he did, he just couldn't seem to avoid hurting the guy's feelings.

He just hoped that this particular faux pas didn't come back to haunt him.

The next day at work, Steven called Robin several times without getting through to her. When he had arrived at his office and turned on his computer, a graphic that read "HELLO, STEVEN—HAVE A WONDERFUL DAY" appeared on the screen instead of his usual screen saver. His secretary must have been feeling a little puckish today and thrown it on there before he came in.

He looked at the message as he dialed Robin's work number for the fifth time. And, for the fifth straight time, he got her voicemail. What, was she avoiding him? "Robin, it's Steven again," he said into the telephone. "I'm still trying to reach you. Okay, I'm at work. Call me."

Frustrated, he hung up the phone and put his head on his desk for a while. Romantic turbulence just didn't agree with him.

The door opened, and his boss stuck his head in without entering.

"How's it going?" Hal asked, sounding more suspicious than casual.

Steven lifted his head and forced himself to smile. "Good," he said.

Hal frowned at him for a long minute. "Going good?" he repeated.

"*Great*," Steven promised with extra gusto. "It's going great."

"Good," Hal said, although he clearly wasn't convinced. "Keep it up."

As he left, Steven's telephone rang.

"Robin on line two," his secretary Joan said over the intercom.

Steven's face lit up and he started to grab the receiver. Then he stopped, took a deep breath, and picked it up more calmly.

"Hey, hi! How you doing? I had the best time the other night," he gushed. "When am

I going to see you again?"

"Well, tonight's not looking too good," the Cable Guy's voice answered. "How about tomorrow?"

The Cable Guy?! How had that happened? It was supposed to be Robin. "Chip?" Steven asked uncertainly.

The Cable Guy, who was cruising around in his van between jobs, laughed into his cellular phone. "I knew I'd get you on the phone that way," he explained.

By *lying*? What kind of guy would pull a trick like that on someone who he knew was heartbroken? Steven didn't answer, not sure if he should yell at the Cable Guy—or his secretary, for cooperating with the sham.

"Listen," the Cable Guy went on, his voice breaking up slightly as he apparently drove past a hill or something. "That equipment will be history soon. Let's go nuts with that karaoke machine."

"What do you mean?" Steven asked, still upset that it wasn't Robin calling him back. How many voicemail messages was he going to have to leave her anyway? Ten? Twenty? A hundred?

"Tomorrow night, karaoke jam," the Cable Guy said. "No ifs, ands, or buts." Then he snickered. "Later, gator!"

Before Steven could argue, he heard the dial tone blaring in his ear.

Well, it looked as though he was having a party tomorrow night—whether he wanted to or not.

# Chapter Eight

Steven was pretty sure that none of his friends would be too excited about singing karaoke all night, so the only person he invited to the party was Rick. After a lot of persuasion, followed by some outright begging, Rick finally agreed to come, as long as Steven promised that he wouldn't have to sing—or even pretend to be a good sport.

The Cable Guy, on the other hand, arrived with a boisterous crowd of about twenty people, most of whom it would be fair to describe as misfits. Steven couldn't quite put his finger on exactly why it was, but all of these people definitely seemed—well, odd.

Within no time at all, the party was in full,

if peculiar, swing. Everyone was in the living room, dancing and mingling, except for Rick, who stood by the window, looking acutely uncomfortable. A terribly skinny, lantern-jawed man stood on the makeshift stage the Cable Guy had set up on the stairs, singing with inept intensity as "American Woman" played on the karaoke machine.

Steven was in the kitchen, refilling bowls of dip and chips. The party seemed to be going pretty well, so he decided to give Robin another call and try to get her to come over. He picked up the telephone and dialed her number.

While it rang, he balanced the receiver on one shoulder of his dinner jacket, so that he could keep opening fresh bags of potato and taco chips. Every so often, one of the misfits would come in, nod at him, and grab another drink from the large supply in the refrigerator.

"Hey, Robin," he said, when she finally answered. "What's up? Did you get my message?"

Robin, who was all dressed up and on her way out, didn't sound all that happy to hear from him. "Yes," she said, rather grimly. "You left me *five* messages. It kind of freaked me out."

When it came to obsessional behavior, five messages were nothing, compared to *eleven* messages. "Sorry," he apologized, shaking his head when one of the misfits offered him another drink. "I've been trying to reach you, 'cause I'm kind of having a party." At this point, it wasn't just a party; it was a bash. "It's a—karaoke . . . jam . . . party," he admitted. "Anyway, you've got to come over."

Robin paused long enough to listen to the noisy music thumping and atonal singing in the background for a moment before answering. "I can't," she said hastily. "I'm going to dinner with someone."

"Dinner?" Steven asked, his jealousy radar perking up. "What, like a date?"

She hesitated again, clearly reluctant to answer. "No. Not really a date."

So it *was* a date! "You've got a date?!" he said, both hurt and angry. As far as he knew, their "trial separation" hadn't included the traditional "see other people" part. "I thought we had fun the other night."

"We did," she agreed, her voice strained. "But that doesn't mean we're officially back together. You said it yourself, time apart is good."

He'd said it, but he'd been lying. "Yes, time apart from each other, but not with other people," Steven said. "I mean, give me a break, that's not time apart; that's time with someone *else*!"

Robin sighed. "I'm not going to do anything, Steven. It's just dinner."

Yeah. Sure. As if "just dinner" couldn't lead to a whole lot more. "Well, what if you like him?" Steven wanted to know, aware that he sounded very petulant. "You might like him better than me." He shook his head. "I can't believe it. This is *so* unfair."

"You're allowed to go out with someone if you want to," she pointed out.

"But *I* don't want to," he said. "We're supposed to be alone, thinking about the other person. I didn't agree to this."

There was a long silence on the other end of the phone. "Fine," she answered. "Then I won't go."

Except that if she stayed home, she would hold it against him, and bring it up during every fight they had for the next twenty years. "No, you have to go," Steven said with a heavy sigh, "because if I say don't, then you'll call me a control freak, and I'm not."

"No, I'm cancelling," Robin said.

Steven shook his head more vehemently even though he knew she couldn't see him. "No, you're *going*," he told her firmly. "I'm not gonna have this pinned on *me*."

She let out her breath, giving up. "All right then. Fine. I'm going."

"Good," he answered, trying not to grind

his teeth together. "Have fun."

"I will," Robin said stiffly.

Yeah, she probably *would*. And *he* wouldn't. Especially as he had visions of her hanging all over some other guy.

After saying a terse good-bye, Steven hung up. As he stood there, scowling at the telephone, the Cable Guy appeared behind him and gave him a drink.

"This is just a sign that you need to live a little," the Cable Guy theorized. "She's having fun, and you should, too."

Steven nodded "Yeah," he said. "You're probably right."

"You know I'm right," the Cable Guy agreed. "I know this stuff."

Steven reached for a small gift-wrapped box on the counter. "Oh, here," he said and handed it to him. "I got you a little something."

The Cable Guy bit his lip. "Wait, I thought you said we were even. You're breaking the rules."

Steven shrugged. "So shoot me," he said.

The Cable Guy tore the wrapping paper from the box, overwhelmed with excitement. "What is it? What is it?" he asked eagerly.

The gift was a self-help cassette entitled "Lose Your Lisp in Thirty Days." Steven's brother Pete had highly recommended it. The

Cable Guy stared at the tape, so moved that he couldn't speak.

"My brother said it might help with your lisp," Steven explained, uncertain of the reaction the Cable Guy would have to this.

The Cable Guy held his gaze for a minute and then hugged him as hard as he could.

"Words cannot express . . ." He shook his head, too overcome by emotion to finish his sentence. "Oh man, you are just too much, I don't deserve this."

Steven shrugged self-consciously. "Don't worry, it's no big deal."

"Yes, it is," the Cable Guy insisted. Then he stared at him until Steven began to squirm a little from embarrassment. "Now I'm on a mission," the Cable Guy announced. "This has got to be the best karaoke jam ever!"

Now Steven relaxed enough to smile back at him. It was always nice to give a present to someone who appreciated it so much.

They went out to the living room, where everyone seemed to be having a great time. It seemed much more crowded now, so more guests must have arrived while Steven was on the phone with Robin. There were even a couple of off-duty cops, who were still in full uniform, singing and dancing along with the rest of the crowd.

"You've got some nice friends!" Steven

yelled over the thumping bass of the music.

The Cable Guy waved that notion aside. "These people are *acquaintances*," he said dismissively. "They're not ride-to-the-airport friends, like us."

Up on the stairs, an older man was singing "Rock the Boat" very badly, but the partygoers were dancing energetically to the beat anyway. In an attempt to make the atmosphere even more festive, the Cable Guy left Steven, grabbed a camera, and began snapping candid pictures of everyone.

He saw Rick slouching by the window and instantly took a Polaroid picture of him. Rick was blinded by the unexpected flash of light and started blinking furiously and rubbing his eyes.

"I'm glad you accepted my invitation," the Cable Guy said cheerily.

Rick shrugged, looking irritated. "Steven invited me, not you."

The Cable Guy gazed over at Steven, who was dancing wildly. "Look at him," he said fondly. "Have you ever seen him so alive? He's changing, Rick. You've got to learn to live with that."

Rick just rolled his eyes. "Yeah, whatever you say. Look, I don't know what your story is, 'Chip Douglas,' but I'm going to find out."

The Cable Guy took a step backwards, pretending to be scared. "Oooh," he said, and made his hands tremble. Then he stepped closer. "Don't dig too deep, you might get burned by the molten lava."

"That's it," Rick said. "I'm out of here."

"Do you want your picture?" the Cable Guy asked, then laughed when Rick didn't respond. "I don't blame you."

Fed up with this whole scene—and Steven's new friends—Rick headed for the front door. He left, slamming the door behind him.

Steven didn't even notice that he was gone.

As the song ended, the Cable Guy tossed Rick's picture into the air and started clapping. "My turn!" he said, and hustled over to the karaoke area. He picked up the microphone and tapped sharply on the receiver to get everyone's attention.

All of the conversations and dancing stopped, and the happy guests looked up at the stairs.

"Raoul, I heard honey in that voice," the Cable Guy said, with the confidence of a professional disc jockey. "First of all, I'd like to thank Steven for being such a terrific host."

Steven smiled and half-waved at the crowd as they applauded.

"Don't forget to kick in some spinach for the food," the Cable Guy reminded them. "Steven ain't made of money, you know what I'm saying? And I expect some of you to join in the clean-up crew."

"Sing something!" one of the off-duty cops yelled. "Do a song!"

The Cable Guy ducked his head with false coyness. "No . . ." he said shyly. "I really couldn't."

"Come on!" the lantern-jawed gaunt guy urged him. "Do your song!"

The Cable Guy was very easy to convince. "Well—all right," he said benevolently. "All right already! I fought the law, and the law won. You might have heard this song performed by the Jefferson Airplane on a little rockumentary called *Gimme Shelter* about the Rolling Stones nightmare at Altamont. That night, a bunch of bikers had their way." He paused for effect. "Tonight, it's *my* turn."

Everyone clapped, then settled back to enjoy his performance. The Cable Guy fiddled with the karaoke machine, and then began to sing "Somebody to Love." What he lacked in talent, he made up in dogged enthusiasm and wild dance moves.

Steven shook his head, amused by the Cable Guy's musical antics. Then he found himself swallowed up again by the crowd.

Up on the karaoke stage, the Cable Guy was singing his heart out. The instrumental section started, and the Cable Guy danced a wild, interpretive dance and ad-libbed to the audience who was clapping and cheering to encourage him.

"We just had a baby born on the left side of the party, ladies and gentlemen," he told them, parodying Woodstock. "We need an ambulance over by the scaffolding. Don't eat the green cheesies! They'll blow your mind."

It had been a wild and crazy night. When Steven woke up the next morning, he wandered into his kitchen. He looked a little disheveled, and felt weary despite a few hours' sleep.

The Cable Guy was standing in front of the stove, cooking breakfast. "Good morning, Mary Sunshine!" he chirped. "And how are we today?"

Steven felt too wasted to answer. He simply poured himself a cup of coffee.

"Hope you don't mind I borrowed your sweatshirt," the Cable Guy said. Steven shrugged.

The Cable Guy turned back to the stove. "Bacon and eggs coming right up," he promised.

Steven sat down at the table with his coffee. He looked around the room, taking in the mess that was left from the karoake jam.

The Cable Guy brought over the frying pan

to serve him his breakfast. "I thought this was all going to get cleaned up," Steven said.

"Oh, but it will, it will," the Cable Guy grinned. "Just give it a little time."

Steven grumbled—and then something caught his eye. He jumped up from the table and ran over to the counter.

"What's this doing here?" he yelled, hauling a thoroughly ruined photograph out of a glass of water.

"Oh, that," the Cable Guy said, whipping up some more eggs. "That little thing? A friend of mine knocked it on the floor, and the frame broke. Then someone poured punch on it. I thought stuffing it in that glass overnight would help wash it off."

Steven was shocked. This was his favorite picture of him and Robin—back when they had started going together. There was no way to replace it. And now it was ruined, stuck in a glass of water all night, because the Cable Guy, in his totally crazy way, had thought he was *helping out*.

"Y-you thought the photo would get *clean* that way!? Look at it! It's like *tissue paper*!! Steven crumpled up the photo. "You're completely nuts!!"

The Cable Guy suddenly realized he might have made a mistake. "Now wait just a second," he frowned. "I can take care of this. Everything's going to be okay."

"I don't want your help," Steven replied, steering him out of the kitchen and towards the exit. "I just want you out of my apartment!" He gestured towards the television and the rest of the entertainment center. "And get all that stuff out of here too. Now!"

The Cable Guy started crying. "Why are you doing this?" he asked through his tears. "You need to ask yourself why you are doing this."

"Get *out*," Steven said through his teeth.

"Why does this always happen?" the Cable Guy asked plaintively. "Everything was going so well. I made you breakfast. We were eating Scrambie eggs!" He gulped his sobs back and looked at Steven pleadingly. "Really—I'll make everything good again."

"Out!" Steven yelled, and pushed him out the door.

"It's okay, I'll fix the photo," the Cable Guy promised.

"Out, *now*!" Steven barked.

The Cable Guy walked unhappily out the door. As soon as he was in the hall, Steven slammed the door shut and triple-locked it.

If he *never* saw the Cable Guy again for the rest of his life—it would be much too soon.

Out in the hall, the Cable Guy's face lit up as he thought of a plan to win his friend back.

"You just relax," he said confidently, speaking through the door. "Everything's *cool*. I'll just let you calm down. I'm leaving your orange juice right outside the door. I'll see you later, okay?"

Steven peeked through the peephole, then opened the door carefully. He reached down to pick up the orange juice—just as the Cable Guy popped out from around the corner.

"This is just a speed bump, Steven," he explained frantically. "Relationships are difficult, don't take this so seriously. This is just a blip. I have so much."

Steven stared at him. The guy was a total loon.

"I have something to say," the Cable Guy insisted. "Listen to me. I just want to reason with you. Okay? Just let me talk. I don't want to freak you out."

With that, Steven slammed the door in his face.

If the Cable Guy didn't want to freak him out, it was too late!

# Chapter Nine

That night, Robin had another date. She and Steven had been together for so long that she had almost forgotten what it was like to date other men. But all things considered, she was willing to learn.

She and her date, Ray, had agreed to have supper at a very fancy local restaurant. The date had been set up by a friend of hers in the art department at *Sassy*, who admitted that she didn't know much about Ray—except that he was *very* handsome.

It was a start.

When Robin and Ray walked into the restaurant together, the Cable Guy was watching from his van, which was parked just down the street. In an attempt to win back Steven's friendship, he had decided that he had to figure out a way to get him back together with Robin. Following her and derailing any dates she had seemed like the best plan.

After a few minutes, he got out of the van and headed for the restaurant entrance. A slim, dark-haired hostess dressed in an elegant black suit came over to greet him.

"May I help you?" she asked.

The Cable Guy shook his head. "No, I'm meeting someone here."

The hostess nodded and withdrew.

The Cable Guy scanned the restaurant until he located Robin, sitting with the same handsome, chiseled man at a table near the window. Her callous lack of fidelity to his best friend in the whole world was very upsetting to him, and after taking a moment to form a plan, he strode directly to the Men's Room.

The restaurant was upscale enough to have attendants in the restrooms, and the Cable Guy saw an older man in neat white pants and a crisply pressed blue shirt standing patiently in front of the sinks.

Another man was washing his hands at the middle sink. The attendant waited until he was finished and then gave him some paper towels. The man dried his hands, deposited the paper towels in a trash can, and then dropped a tip in the small wicker basket on the sink counter.

"Most appreciated," the bathroom attendant said politely as the man left.

The Cable Guy walked over to him and dramatically whipped out a twenty-dollar bill.

"You've been working too hard," he said, holding the money out. "Take a break."

The attendant grinned, glanced around to make sure that no one else was watching, and then tucked the money away in his shirt pocket. "Most appreciated, sir," he answered.

The Cable Guy smiled and rubbed his hands together with anticipation.

As soon as Robin's date needed to use the facilities, the Cable Guy was going to . . . *attend* . . . to him.

Sitting out in the restaurant, Robin and Ray were having a somewhat stilted conversation as they ate their salads. Ray was indeed extremely handsome, but he was, perhaps, somewhat less gifted in the area of mental acuity. For twenty minutes now he had been telling her at length about his greatest ambition in life.

"My brother and I wanna start our own sunblock company," he said, his eyes shining with excitement. "But the twist is, it's only for *skiing*. Sunski."

"Sunski?" Robin repeated, and ate some arugula.

"SkiBlock," Ray went on, his eyes faraway. "Or . . . SunSki. We haven't decided yet." He frowned. "Maybe *BlockSki*. Do you think that sounds good?"

"BlockSki?" Robin asked, glancing at him for confirmation. "Oh. Well—that sounds right."

Ray nodded, delighted by his own incredible business acumen. He speared a small tomato rose on the tip of his fork, and smiled knowingly at her. "So," he said, and popped the tomato into his mouth. "Gail told me you're just coming off a relationship."

She didn't want to give him any ideas, but she didn't want to lie either. "Well, not really," Robin answered cautiously. "We're in kind of a holding pattern. He wants more of a commitment, but I don't think I'm ready. I just want to have a good time for a while."

"Then we gotta get you on a Ski-Doo!" Ray told her.

Which sounded unusual, to say the very least. "Um, Ski-Doo?" she asked.

"High-powered snowmobile," he explained. "It'll blow your mind. It flies over powder likes it's glass."

And that was a *good* thing? The last she'd heard, snowmobiles raised a number of environmental concerns. "Well," Robin said and ate some endive. "Gosh."

Their waitress was just passing by with a full tray of drinks and Ray snapped his fingers at her repeatedly until she stopped.

"Hey, how are you doing on that chicken?" he asked impatiently. "Have the eggs hatched yet? Thanks."

The waitress set her jaw slightly but moved on without commenting further. Robin, who had waited tables herself during college, was mortified by Ray's behavior.

Looking dissatisfied by the waitress' lack of instant cooperation, Ray grabbed a roll from the breadbasket, buttered it sloppily, and took a large bite. "So," he said. "How's your work going?"

Ray had only been talking about *his* job, and *his* problems, for quite some time now, and it was a pleasant novelty for him to ask her a personal question. "It's been crazy," she answered honestly. "They just hired a—"

"Hold that thought," he interrupted her. "I have to use the restroom. Be right back."

Instead of feeling insulted as he left, Robin was more relieved than anything else. Frankly, she could use a break from him. If she *really* got lucky, he might even forget to come back.

Scurrying past her with another heavily laden tray, the waitress looked relieved too.

When Ray entered the restroom, the Cable Guy was ready and waiting for him. He had swapped outfits with the attendant so he was now snappily attired in the attendant's blue shirt and white pants. He had also provided himself with a thin, fake mustache.

After giving the Cable Guy a tip, a distinguished-looking man was just exiting the restroom when Ray marched confidently inside.

"Enjoy your meal, sir," the Cable Guy said, and the man gave him a friendly wave as he left.

Ray walked towards the stalls.

"Good evening, sir," the Cable Guy said, ducking his head obsequiously, although his voice was a little anxious.

Ray nodded, without making eye contact. "What do you say there, Stretch?"

The Cable Guy coughed to hide his excitement about what was going to happen in the next few minutes. "Pleasant night, isn't it?"

"Yeah," Ray answered curtly. "Not too bad."

"But I guess the weather's always pleasant in here," the Cable Guy went on. "The winters are remarkably mild." Then he laughed loudly at his own joke, slapping his knee several times for emphasis.

Ray didn't even crack a smile as he headed straight for the handicapped stall.

"If you need anything, just let me know," the Cable Guy said from his watchful position next to the sinks. "Anything at all."

Ray looked annoyed. "Don't bother. I've got it covered," he said.

Suddenly, as if out of thin air, the Cable Guy was standing right behind him, so close that Ray was startled.

"Oh, it's no trouble, *really*," the Cable Guy whispered ominously into his ear.

"Man! What the—" Ray tried to push him away with his free hand. "Get out of here!"

"*Most* people never bother to take advantage of all my services," the Cable Guy explained with a demented grin. "For instance . . ."

Deciding to show instead of tell, the Cable Guy grabbed the back of Ray's shirt and kicked his feet out from under him. Then he pulled Ray out of the stall and dragged him over to the sink counter.

"I can help you wash up," the Cable Guy said, as he demonstrated *exactly* what he meant by that. "Cleanliness is next to godliness."

"You're on a big date, you'll need to look your best!" the Cable Guy said. He sprayed Ray in the face with water, smashed him in the face with a powder puff and then pulled out some tweezers. "The monobrow looks good on Bert and Ernie, but not on *you*."

With that, he began to forcibly tweeze Ray's eyebrows, as Ray yelped and tried to get away from him. Once he was finished and Ray's eyebrows were gone, the Cable Guy looked down and studied his efforts thoughtfully.

"Let me do a little Jose Eber on you," he decided, and combed Ray's hair into a very goofy-looking side part. "Jose Eber—with a twist of Alfalfa!"

Ray just stared up at him, his mouth opening and closing in shock.

"Looking good!" the Cable Guy said and winked at him. "And Boom, Bam, we're ready to dry you off."

He rammed Ray face first into the starting button of an automatic hand dryer. The machine turned on with a loud whoosh, and the Cable Guy held Ray's face right up next to the blast of hot air.

"Now suck it," he ordered and shoved him closer. "Suck the air!"

Ray hesitantly put his mouth around the nozzle and his cheeks started fluttering like an astronaut experiencing heavy G-forces.

The Cable Guy watched this phenomenon with a certain amount of fascination.

"From this angle, you look just like Dizzy Gillespie," he remarked, and then started bopping like Dizzy.

Once he was sure that Ray had been properly cowed by this whole experience, the Cable Guy pulled him away from the hand dryer. As he did, Ray's mouth made a popping noise like a suction cup.

"Don't worry about the tip," the Cable Guy said, putting on a sunnily crazed smile. "But I've got one for you." He leaned closer to hiss directly into Ray's ear. "Stay away from Robin. She's *taken*."

Then he opened the restroom door and tossed Ray out to the hallway. Ray hit the floor with a thud and lay there, too stunned to get up.

The Cable Guy smiled. It was always such a good feeling to help out a dear friend who was like a brother to him. He glanced both ways to make sure no one was looking, and then slipped out through the back exit, considering it an evening very well spent.

Out in the restaurant, Robin sat alone at her table and wondered where Ray had gone. Their meals had arrived and were getting very cold. She glanced at her watch, waited some more, and then gave up and dug into her grilled salmon.

It was delicious.

Steven was home alone, watching television and eating a tepid TV dinner. His microwave oven seemed to be on the fritz, so the meal hadn't come out very well. On the positive side, he had thought ahead and bought that brand that included a second helping.

The local news was on, and he watched the usual stories about murder, mayhem, and general societal anarchy without much interest. For some reason though, no matter how disturbing the story was, the anchorpeople never lost their glazed smiles.

"Here's a bizarre story from downtown, where a man was beaten in a restroom by an assailant disguised as a bathroom attendant," the anchorman said after the weatherman had joyfully promised "rain, rain, and *more*—you guessed it—rain!" "The victim has been unable to speak since the unmotivated attack," the anchorman said, dropping his voice to a respectful, if delighted, hush.

Steven watched the image of a shaken-up Ray being led gently out of the restaurant by two police officers to a waiting ambulance. It was really amazing—even restrooms weren't safe anymore.

"A police sketch artist put together this drawing from witnesses' descriptions," the anchorman continued.

An Identikit drawing flashed onto the screen that looked a little like the Cable Guy, except that the man had a mustache and appeared to be Hispanic. As was his duty as a good citizen, Steven stopped chewing and studied the drawing carefully to see if he knew the man. Somehow, he seemed vaguely familiar. But then, Steven decided that he was mistaken and promptly lost interest.

He changed the channel and the UPN logo flew up onto the screen, followed by a slick commercial for a UPN movie-of-the-week about the Sam Sweet trial. It was the third of four movies on the subject that were scheduled to be shown on various stations during sweeps periods. Steven wasn't proud to admit that he had actually watched the first two and been, frankly, engrossed.

"Tonight on UPN," an announcer was saying, "the true story behind the trial that's captured the nation."

The commercial switched to a quick scene from the movie. The clip showed the lead actor, an angry Eric Roberts, holding a shotgun, which he was pointing at another, very scared, Eric Roberts.

"The jury may still be out," the male announcer acknowledged stentoriously, "but the chilling facts are in. Eric Roberts, in his dramatic debut on UPN, *is* Sam and Stan Sweet. *Brother, Sweet Brother: The Killing of Stanton Sweet.* Tonight on UPN."

Steven grinned wryly. That one looked like

a must-skip. He flipped the channel to a college basketball game on ESPN and settled back to enjoy the rest of his undercooked Salisbury steak.

The Cable Guy knew that it wasn't enough simply to shove some lame loser of a date out of Steven's way. He was going to have to do even more to win back his best buddy's undying friendship.

The next morning, he went over to Robin's apartment building at 1268½ Chestnut Street. A woman had just come outside to pick up her daily newspaper, and the Cable Guy walked up to her.

"Excuse me," he said politely. "Apartment 202 is Robin Harris?"

The neighbor nodded and pointed. "It's right upstairs," she answered.

The Cable Guy smiled and took the steps two at a time. With a friendship hanging in the balance, there was no time to waste.

Robin was inside her apartment, rushing to get ready to go to work, when she heard a loud knock on her front door. Since she wasn't expecting anyone, she was instantly wary. After the horror of the night before—it was the first time she had ever dated someone who had been brutally attacked by a total stranger masquerading as a bathroom attendant—she was still feeling pretty shaky.

"Who is it?" she asked through the door.

"It's the Cable Guy," the Cable Guy answered.

Robin frowned skeptically. The cable guys didn't come when you *wanted* them; why would one show up when she *hadn't* even called the company? "There's no problem with my cable," she said.

The Cable Guy cleared his throat, to make his voice deeper, so he would sound more official. "I've got an upgrade order for one Robin Harris. The Rainbow Package," he added and paused to shake his head with admiration. "That's *every* pay channel available."

She had absolutely no interest in receiving the Rainbow Package. This was probably some dumb promotion the company was doing, where they would offer her a free week of premium channels with the hope that she would get hooked and pay dearly to continue receiving the service.

"I'm sorry," Robin said. "I didn't order that."

The Cable Guy chuckled. "Well, apparently you've got a secret admirer."

Secret? Fat chance. Robin opened the door a few inches, but left the chain on. "Was it a man named Steven?" she asked suspiciously. He was just kidding himself if he thought giving her a few crummy movie channels would be enough to make her forgive the way he had been behaving lately.

The Cable Guy's smile was coy. "I'm afraid I can't tell you that."

"Come on," Robin pleaded.

The Cable Guy shook his head. "No, I promised Steven I wouldn't say." Then he stopped abruptly and put his hand over his mouth, feigning embarrassment. "Oh my goodness. What have I done? You didn't hear it from *me*."

Robin opened the door all the way, and the Cable Guy stepped inside.

"What a lovely apartment," he remarked.

"I have to get ready for work," she said impatiently, "so do whatever you have to do."

"You won't even know I'm here," the Cable Guy assured her. "I'm Claude Rains. I'm the Invisible Man." He waved his hands to usher her away. "Go slay the dragon."

Robin smiled in spite of herself and went to go blow-dry her hair.

The Cable Guy climbed up into the air duct, pulling a long length of co-axial cord behind him. When he reached a vent in the duct, he hooked up the cable connection. You could never tell, he thought, when favors like this would be returned.

# Chapter Ten

When Robin had left the room and the coast seemed clear, the Cable Guy dropped down from the closet ceiling. He landed lightly on his feet with his arms outstretched. Russian judges would have given him an 8.5. He walked out to the living room. Robin was checking through the contents of her briefcase one last time before heading to work.

"That about does it," the Cable Guy told her as he brushed a few stray specks of dust from his jumpsuit. Cleanliness was, if not a rule in his life, at least a goal.

Robin nodded, looking up long enough from her papers to flash him a brief smile.

"Okay. Thank you," she said, and snapped her briefcase shut. "So, are you a friend of Steven's?"

The Cable Guy smiled back. "I'm proud to say I am," he answered. "I installed his cable recently, and we just hit it off. We bonded big-time."

This was news to Robin, but then she recalled Steven's describing himself as a "preferred customer" the night the cable had gone out when they were trying to watch *Sleepless in Seattle*. "That's right," she remembered. "You fixed his cable the other night."

"Guilty," the Cable Guy admitted.

"So, uh, you guys are going out *a lot*?" she asked suspiciously.

They weren't spending nearly enough time together, as far as the Cable Guy was concerned. Friends who were like brothers should be inseparable. "Not really," he said. "That man is devoted to you."

*Too* devoted, in Robin's opinion, but she decided not to say so.

The Cable Guy paused, then lowered his voice, even though there was no one else in the apartment to overhear their conversation. "You know, I'm probably crossing a boundary telling you this," he confided, "but he's really crazy about you."

Robin frowned. "Did he say that?"

"Only every five minutes," the Cable Guy chuckled. "Quite frankly, I'm sick of hearing it!" Then he relented. "No, I'm just kidding you." He moved closer so that he could look deep into her eyes. "He's a good man. He mentioned that you guys have had some problems."

*That* was putting it mildly, as far as Robin was concerned. "Well, it's a little complicated," she answered.

The Cable Guy nodded in sympathy. "It always is," he commiserated.

Robin didn't really feel like discussing her romantic debacle with him—or anyone else, for that matter, so she just nodded vaguely, smiled again, and ushered him towards the front door.

"You know, I asked a woman to marry me once," the Cable Guy confessed. "She said she wanted to think about it. We agreed to take some time apart to re-assess our feelings. To give each other . . . *space*," he said, mockingly stressing the word "space." Then he blinked rapidly, brushed his hand across his eyes, and made a visible effort to swallow. "Well, she is no longer with us."

"Oh no. I'm so sorry," Robin told him, meaning every word of it.

The Cable Guy promptly began sobbing. "Sometimes, you don't know what you have, until it's gone. Just—'' He gulped a few times, trying to get himself under control. ''Just promise me you'll never go bungee jumping in Mexico. They *just don't have* the regulations.''

Robin gasped. What a horrible and senseless tragedy this poor man had experienced. ''I promise,'' she said, with heartfelt emotion.

The Cable Guy quickly rubbed his sleeve across his damp eyes, pretending to be embarrassed that he had broken down in front of her like that. ''Anyway,'' he said, his voice thick with unshed tears, ''I've said too much.''

Robin reached out and covered his hand with both of hers. ''Thank you. I *mean* that.''

The Cable Guy managed a tremulous smile. ''Cherish him,'' he said fervently. ''Every hair on his head.''

Then he departed without another word, leaving her alone in the middle of her living room.

Robin stood very still for a moment or two, struck by the truth in what the Cable Guy had told her. It was so easy to take people for granted, and yet life was so very fragile and precious.

Starting today, right here, and right now, she was going to *remember* that.

\* \* \*

Instead of going to his office, Steven was spending the full day on-site at the old school-house his company was going to convert to condominiums. Hal had wanted him to go and supervise the construction workers, at least during the initial phase of the renovation.

He was walking down a long Gothic—and *dusty*—hallway in the school building when his cellular phone rang. He pulled the phone from his jacket pocket and snapped it open with one practiced move of his wrist.

"Hello?" he said, speaking over the noise of the construction behind him.

"I love you," a woman's voice said passionately.

Steven held the phone away from his ear and looked at it uncertainly before putting it back. "Robin?" he asked, not sure if he had heard right.

"Yes," she answered.

"Well, I . . . love you too," he said, still so surprised to hear her voice—to say nothing of the sentiments she had expressed—that he wondered if he could possibly have misunderstood her.

Standing in her apartment, Robin squeezed the telephone receiver tightly. "That was so sweet of you," she said, feeling close to tears.

Steven didn't even have the slightest idea of what was going on here, but he was certainly willing to play along. "Oh . . . well . . ."

"You didn't have to do that," she declared.

Tell her that he loved her? But she already *knew* that; it was one of the reasons they had started fighting in the first place! "I . . . wanted to," he said, still feeling as though he was wandering blindly through this conversation.

"Giving me free cable," she elaborated. "Only you would do something like that. I mean, the *Rainbow* Package? You really shouldn't have, Steven."

Free cable? Well, okay. Why not? "You got it?" he asked. "Great."

"Yes, your friend came by," she said.

Ah. The plot thickened. "My friend?" Steven repeated, hearing his voice stiffen.

"The Cable Guy," Robin said, nodding enthusiastically. "I liked him. He was kind of goofy, but nice. Anyway, thank you so much for doing that."

It would be a whole lot easier to take credit for his thoughtful and expensive gift, if he had actually *given* it to her. "I, uh, I'm glad you liked it," Steven stammered. "I've wanted to do something for you, but I've been trying to give you your space."

"Well, I don't think we should make rules anymore," she said.

That sounded like a good plan to him.

"Okay," he agreed eagerly.

"Call me later if you're around?" she asked.

Steven was so elated by this turn of events that he could barely contain himself. "Sure!" he said. "I'll call you as soon as I get home. Bye." He hung up and stuck the cellular phone back in his pocket.

Wow! What had happened to change her mind? Did it matter? No. All that mattered was that she had changed it, and he was back in her good graces again. Things were definitely looking up!

"Steven, are you ready to rock?" a familiar voice asked from behind him.

Steven turned to see Rick, who was wearing a Soundgarden T-shirt. Realizing that he had already made plans tonight with Rick, Steven closed his eyes for a second.

"Right. The concert," he said, then winced. "Oh man."

"What?" Rick asked. "Come on, let's go. It's going to be hard enough to find a parking place as it is." Then he saw Steven's expression. "What?" he asked again, sounding much less friendly.

Steven sighed. "Robin just called. I-I think we're getting back together."

At first, Rick looked confused, but then he caught on. "So wait," Rick said, clearly annoyed. "You're blowing me off?" He shook his head. "I can't believe this."

"This is the first time *she* asked to get to-gether," Steven said in his own defense, although it sounded like kind of a lame excuse to him too.

Rick glared at him, standing with his hands on his hips. "You do this every time, you know that? You only call me after a girl breaks your heart." Then he imitated Steven's voice, perfectly capturing his inflections. " 'Oh, Rick, can I stay on your couch? Let's talk all night about how mean girls are.' *Then*, as soon as you find another girl, you blow me off." He shook his head in disgust. "I really don't know why I fall for it anymore."

Steven just shrugged weakly. It was kind of an unfortunate little pattern he had going there.

To make matters even worse, when they got outside to the old schoolhouse's parking lot, Steven's car wouldn't start and Rick had to drive him home.

It was pouring out, and they didn't speak once during the entire ride. Every time Steven would start to say something, Rick would just glare angrily at him and then stare straight ahead. The only sound was the windshield wipers swinging back and forth.

Rick pulled up in front of Steven's building

and waited silently for him to get out of the car.

"Don't be mad," Steven said. Begged, really. "Can't you get someone else to use the ticket?"

"Yeah," Rick said, and scowled at him. "Maybe I'll get *my* cable guy to go!"

Since it was pretty obvious that Rick wasn't going to forgive him any time soon, Steven got out of the car. Then Rick drove away without even glancing back.

Great. Now his best friend hated him. Steven slogged through the rain, not even bothering to check his mail on the way to his apartment. It would probably just be bills, and besides, he really didn't care right now.

He was walking up the outside staircase leading to his apartment, hanging on the railing, when the Cable Guy jumped out from behind a corner.

"Pretty smooth work," the Cable Guy said happily. "I set 'em up, you knock 'em down."

Steven didn't know what he was talking about, and he didn't feel like hearing an explanation, either. "What?" he asked, fumbling for his keys.

"*Robin*," the Cable Guy reminded him. "I got her back for you. I juiced her up."

So what? He was the one Robin loved, after all. "Oh, yeah? How do you know we're back together?" he asked without much interest.

The Cable Guy shrugged, indicating that the answer was self-evident. "Are you kidding? Free cable is the *ultimate* love potion."

"Yeah, well, I don't want you messing around with my life," Steven said. "Okay?"

The Cable Guy looked unhappy. "I felt bad about the other night, so I wanted to make it up to you." With that out of the way, his expression brightened. "So anyway. What are you doing? Do you want to catch a flick?"

Steven turned to look at him. Could anyone really be that dense? He would try to let the guy down easily, but it was really time for him to take the hint and go away. "Look," he said patiently, as though he were trying to reason with a small and not terribly intelligent child. "I appreciate you helping me out with Robin. Really."

The Cable Guy nodded, his eyes puppylike in their eagerness to be liked.

"But you have to understand," Steven went on. "I'm going to have to work extra hard to not screw this relationship up again."

The Cable Guy nodded earnestly, in full agreement with that.

Now came the hard part. "You're very nice," Steven assured him, "but I just don't have any room in my life for a new friend. Okay?"

The Cable Guy looked puzzled. "What are you trying to say?"

"I don't want to be your friend," Steven said kindly, but firmly.

The Cable Guy's eyes widened, but then he just started nodding. "Oh. Okay. I get it." He backed a few steps away. "No problem. I appreciate your honesty. You're a real straight shooter."

Somehow, he hadn't expected it to be that easy. He had been prepared for begging, pleading, and maybe even some wailing and gnashing of teeth. "So you're all right?" Steven asked tentatively.

"Hey, I'm a big boy," the Cable Guy said. "It's no big deal. Whatever."

Well—good. What a relief. "You sure?" Steven asked, checking one last time.

The Cable Guy nodded. "Oh, I'm fine."

Since there wasn't much else to say, Steven walked the rest of the way up the stairs to his apartment. Then he unlocked the door and went inside.

The Cable Guy just stood there, alone and unhappy, in the pouring rain.

That night, Robin came over to Steven's apartment. They spent a quiet evening together, talking softly and hugging every so often. Steven had put flickering candles on the coffee table and the mantlepiece. After a while, the mood got more romantic, and they cuddled up on the couch.

The television was on, and Conan O'Brien was doing a monologue about Sam Sweet and the "Twin Envy" trial that was apparently never going to end. The Cable Guy still hadn't shown up to take all of the new electronic equipment away, and although Steven wouldn't have admitted it, he was really enjoying having the stuff around. It was top-quality all the way.

As Conan's monologue continued, Steven and Robin started kissing. Outside, it was still raining, and there were occasional flashes of lightning and cracks of thunder. Somehow, the storm just made their reunion seem all the more passionate.

In the middle of one long kiss, there was a blinding flash of lightning and Steven instinctively looked up—just in time to see the Cable Guy staring down at them, with his face pressed against the skylight.

Steven gasped, but when the lightning flashed again, there was no one there. Had it been real, or had he just been imagining his worst nightmare?

Seeing how scared he looked, Robin rested her hand against his cheek. "What is it?" she asked, sounding worried. "Are you all right?"

Was he? Or was he seeing things? "Uh, I'm fine," Steven said hastily, and they went back to kissing.

With luck, he wasn't losing his mind.

# Chapter Eleven

The Cable Guy made a point of calling Robin at her office early the next morning. Instead of doing something more traditional—like, oh, say using a pay phone—he was on top of a telephone pole, strapped in with a safety belt and dressed as a phone company employee. He had illegally hooked a repairman's phone into the wiring, and the reception was just fabulous. Even though it would be a little inconvenient, he might have to start making all of his phone calls this way.

"Hey, it's Chip Douglas," he said, when Robin answered the call.

"Chip Douglas?" she asked, obviously not recognizing his name.

Well, that was some lousy memory *she* had. And here he was, thinking that he'd made an unforgettable impression on her. Why would Steven fall for someone who was so addled? "Your cable guy," the Cable Guy prompted her.

"Oh, hi," she said, sounding surprised to hear from him. "What's up?"

"I feel kind of weird calling you," he lied. Actually, he felt perfectly fine about it, but women liked men who admitted to occasional bouts of shyness—he'd seen it on Ricki Lake once. "It's just . . ." He paused for effect. "I'm worried about Steven."

"What is it?" she asked, concerned. Steven had seemed perfectly fine when she'd left. In fact, he had been in a noticeably terrific mood.

The Cable Guy sighed. "I don't know. Something isn't right. He hasn't been himself lately. Have you noticed anything?"

Robin gave that some thought. If she were to pick one word to describe Steven's frame of mind, she would have gone with "ebullient." "No," she said slowly. "Things are actually going really well."

"Oh. Good," the Cable Guy said in a distinctly funereal tone.

"Should I be worried?" Robin asked.

He let a foreboding pause pass before responding. "Nope," he said. "I'm probably just being a nervous nellie. Let's just keep our eyes open."

"I will," Robin answered nervously. "Thank you for calling me. Good-bye."

Steven really *had* seemed just fine to her, so maybe she hadn't been paying close enough attention, or—on this other hand, he and his cable guy had become such good friends lately, so who would know how Steven was really feeling, if not the Cable Guy?

The only thing to do was to call Steven right away and make sure he was okay. She wouldn't be able to relax until she had spoken to him.

Even during their separation, she hadn't taken his office number off her speed dial, so she pressed that button and the call quickly went through.

"Steven Kovacs, please," she said, trying to control her uneasiness.

"Oh, hi, Robin," his secretary, Joan, answered. "Sorry, he's in a meeting."

"Could you have him call me as soon as he gets free?" Robin asked. "It's—" She shouldn't say that it was an emergency, exactly, but it *was* urgent. "Please just tell him it's really important."

"Sure thing," Joan promised.

Robin hung up and then sat nervously at her desk, waiting for him to call back.

Until he did, she knew she wouldn't be able to concentrate on anything else.

In the meantime, Steven was sitting in the conference room at a sales meeting about the schoolhouse development deal. Only about a dozen of the top employees at the company had been invited to this meeting, and Steven was very pleased that Hal Daniels had included him. Maybe there really *was* a promotion in his not-too-distant future.

The most senior sales manager at Citywide Land Developers was standing at the front of the room, giving a presentation about the initial stages of the deal. So far, the deal didn't seem to have any downside at all.

"The response to our initial offering has been remarkable," the sales manager said, gesturing to a graph that illustrated the sales potential of the project. "A local investment group has decided to buy the entire complex and turn them into rentals."

Steven listened intently to all of this. So far, his plan seemed to be working even more successfully than he would have predicted in his wildest dreams.

"In retrospect, I must admit we made one big mistake," the sales manager said.

Steven stiffened in his chair, prepared to hear some serious criticism, while his coworkers also hung on the sales manager's every word.

The sales manager grinned. "We should have asked for more money."

Now everyone in the room laughed. When the amusement finally died down, Mr. Daniels got up from his seat and smiled at Steven.

"I just want to put this out there, Stevey," he said, and raised a proud fist in the air. "You did it, man. You laid your cards, and mine, out on the table—and you slam-dunked it. Way to go!"

In response to that, the rest of the employees in the room started clapping.

"Now watch, they'll give him *my* job," Mr. Daniels joked nervously.

This time, no one quite had the nerve to laugh, although there were plenty of discreet coughs.

"All right, on to other business," Mr. Daniels said, returning to his normal brusque efficiency. "We have just closed escrow on the downtown plot. So, now that *that* bear is off our back, we can get down to the business of finding an architect."

Steven took out a blank lined pad so that he could take notes.

"Corporate has sent over a list," Mr. Daniels said, and waved a piece of paper. "I don't know where they come up with these people, but I'm going to recommend that we go with the guys over at Sulley and Richfield. They've done this job before, and Bill is a golfing buddy. They're definitely going to deliver."

As Mr. Daniels continued speaking, Joan tried to get Steven's attention from a crack in the door.

"Pssst," she hissed. "Steven."

Steven turned slightly and saw her motioning for him to come out to the hall. In the middle of an executive-level meeting? Not a chance. What was she thinking? He waved her off impatiently.

"Steven, I *really* need to speak with you," she whispered urgently.

Some of the people around the conference table were beginning to notice this exchange, and Steven looked very uncomfortable.

"It can wait," Steven muttered curtly.

Right then, two police officers stormed into the room, while Joan stood behind them with a concerned expression on her face.

"Is there a Steven Kovacs here?" one of the officers demanded.

Everyone at the table turned to look at Steven. He flushed, and raised his hand slightly.

"Uh . . . I'm Steven Kovacs," he admitted, wondering what this could possibly be about. Were they here because he'd "lost" his last jury duty summons? "What's going on?"

The other, taller officer took out a pair of handcuffs. "You're under arrest," he said.

Everyone gasped, including Steven.

"What did he do?" Mr. Daniels asked.

"Receipt of stolen merchandise," the first officer said shortly.

Steven stared at the two cops. "What?! I never—"

"Do not speak until spoken to," the same cop ordered.

Instinctively, Steven made a sudden move in the police officer's direction, and the cop jabbed him sharply in the ribs with his night stick. Steven groaned in pain and leaned over, clutching his side.

The cop kicked his legs apart, and started frisking him in front of everyone. Steven submitted to the search, his face bright red with humiliation.

"Hands behind your back," the officer barked, once the search for weapons had been completed.

Silently, Steven did as he was told. The taller officer cuffed his wrists roughly together, and then spun him around to face them.

"You have the right to remain silent," he read from a small card.

Oh great, he was being *Mirandized* now. Steven closed his eyes.

"Anything you say may be used against you in a court of law," the officer went on, as at least half of the people in the room—well-schooled from years of watching television—mouthed the words along with him. "You have the right to an attorney. If you cannot afford an attorney, one will be provided for you." Then he put the card away. "Do you understand these rights as I have given them to you?"

"This is all a mistake," Steven insisted. "I didn't accept any stolen goods."

But just then, it hit him, and he heard the Cable Guy's voice in his head, saying, "You're getting THX-quality sound that would make George Lucas a very happy camper." He realized that all of that sound and video equipment really *might* have been stolen.

The police officers shoved him towards the door, and Steven glanced back at his coworkers' horrified faces as he was taken away.

"Hey, relax," he said, trying to break the tension with a joke. "*I'm* the one who's going to jail."

Nobody laughed, particularly Mr. Daniels.

The two police officers walked Steven out of the office tower and downstairs to a waiting police car.

As they stepped outside, there was a man standing across the street, pretending to look under the upraised hood of his car. It was the Cable Guy, covertly watching Steven's humiliation.

As one of the cops pushed Steven into the back seat of the car, he glanced over at the Cable Guy and touched the side of his nose, the same way Paul Newman and Robert Redford had in *The Sting*.

It was their pre-arranged signal, and the Cable Guy solemnly touched his nose in return.

Naturally, *he* was the confidential informant who had given the stolen merchandise tip to the police in the first place. It might not have been a very nice thing to do for him, but by rejecting his loving friendship, Steven had simply left him no choice.

Steven had never been arrested before, and he found the whole experience incredibly unpleasant, to say nothing of embarrassing. Although he hated to do it, he gave in and used his one call to telephone his father. It went without saying that his father was *not* happy to hear from him under those circumstances.

An hour later, his father, Earl, appeared at the station, with their family lawyer in tow. All of the interrogation and witness rooms were occupied, so they had to sit on a wooden bench in the public hallway to discuss the situation. Steven was chained to the bench, since the police apparently thought he would try to escape otherwise.

Earl shook his head unhappily. "I can't *believe* you did this," he said for the tenth time.

"But *I* didn't do anything, Dad," Steven insisted. "Honest."

Hearing that—also for the tenth time—his father looked irritated. "Come on, Steven," he chided his son. "He gave you a big-screen TV and a hi-fi system as a *present*? You expect me to believe that?" He shook his head. "You know, you're killing your mother with this."

The first thing his father had said when he arrived was that his mother had been too overcome by the bad news to accompany him to the precinct house. Right now, presumably, she was lying down in their bedroom with the shades drawn. Steven sighed. "I swear it's true, Dad."

"Why would you even accept such extravagant gifts?" his father wanted to know.

Good question. "I don't know," Steven said frankly. In any case, it had been an incredibly stupid thing to do. "I shouldn't have."

Earl frowned, and Steven could tell that he found that excuse pretty lame.

"What is really going on here, Steven?" his father asked sternly. "Can you tell me that? Are you on something? Are you doing something wrong?"

Steven had to fight off a smile, since his father hadn't exactly entered the 1990s yet. He'd missed the 1960s, the 1970s, and the 1980s too. Somehow, he was still mired back in the 1950s.

"I'm fine," Steven maintained. "And—I didn't do anything!"

"Mmmm," was his father's only tight-lipped response.

There was no way he was going to be able to get through to his father when he was this angry, so Steven turned towards his glumly silent lawyer instead. "Please, call my cable guy, his name is Ernie Douglas."

The lawyer shook his head pessimistically. "Steven, the police looked into it. Nobody named Ernie Douglas works for the cable company."

Steven stared at him. "What?"

"Sorry," his lawyer said with a helpless shrug. "They checked."

Steven was going to rest his head in his hands, but the chains were too short, so he settled for slouching lower on the bench, instead.

"Well, that's just *wonderful*. You want to tell us the truth now?" his father asked.

Of course there was a cable guy named Ernie Douglas; there *had* to be. Suddenly overwhelmed by everything, Steven felt himself falling apart. "That's got to be a mistake," he said, almost crying. "Oh, this isn't happening."

"Yes it is," his father answered furiously, "and it's killing your mother."

Yeah, well, it wasn't doing *him* much good, either.

"Tell me something. Did you *deliberately* want to ruin our fortieth anniversary party on Monday, Steven?" his father wanted to know.

"Yeah, Dad, I did," Steven said sarcastically. "It's all a big plan." He glanced over at his lawyer. "When can you get me out of here?"

His lawyer shifted his position, looking acutely uncomfortable. "I'm sorry," he said. "Unfortunately it's too late to get a bail hearing today. You're going to have to spend the weekend in county lockup."

Steven groaned loudly. An already disastrous situation had just become *significantly* worse.

*   *   *

Once all of the paperwork had been completed and Steven had been photographed, finger-printed, and booked, he was driven over to the local prison in a police van. After being searched extensively and forced to shower with lice-killing shampoo, he was issued a pair of prison blues, a lumpy pillow, and a set of dingy sheets.

Two guards led him down the long corridor to his cell. Lining each side of the hall were other cells, filled with angry prisoners. As Steven walked by, keeping his eyes straight ahead, the prisoners taunted him and threw things out of their cells. It was one of his worst nightmares come to living, breathing, *noisy* life.

"Hey everybody!" one of the prisoners yelled gleefully. "Look at him!"

"Oh, is baby scared?!" another prisoner cooed threateningly. "Don't cry, baby!"

The prisoners all kept laughing and scream-ing at him until he finally reached his cell. One of the guards unlocked the door and Steven stepped inside.

The guard closed the door with a loud metallic slam and then locked it. As Steven heard the key turning in the lock, he shut his eyes. This really *was* the worst thing he could imagine.

Hearing something move behind him,

Steven turned to see a muscle-bound, angry-looking prisoner standing inside the cell with him.

His cellmate. His extremely *nasty* cellmate.

Steven sighed, and slouched back against the wall. So far, this really had not been a red-letter day.

Steven decided that it would be the better part of wisdom to sleep with his eyes open that night. To his chagrin, he also—much like Mary Richards—found himself wanting nothing more than to brush his teeth.

Shortly after eating a very mediocre breakfast and standing in a long line for a head-count, a grouchy guard appeared at his cell door to tell him that his lawyer had arrived to visit him.

Steven jumped off his bunk and followed the guard eagerly down to the reception room, excited to hear any news about how his case was going.

His lawyer was sitting on the other side of the glass, with his back to Steven. Steven sat down on a small metal stool that was bolted to the floor, and picked up the telephone to speak to him.

"What did you hear?" he demanded. "Did you hear anything yet?"

The man turned around, and Steven's face

fell. It wasn't his lawyer, but rather—why was he surprised?—the Cable Guy, dressed in an expensive suit.

"Hello, Steven," he said formally. "I came as soon as I heard."

Steven slouched forward and rested his head on his arms for a minute. If he promised to stop watching television for the rest of his life, maybe he would wake up and find out that none of this had ever happened.

The Cable Guy looked offended. "Aren't you happy to see me?"

Oh yeah, he was overjoyed. "Who are you?" Steven asked. "What's your real name?"

The Cable Guy shook his head, avoiding the questions. "That's not important right now," he said. "We have to get you out of here." He glanced both ways, and then leaned forward. "I was watching Court TV, and I think I found a loophole in your case. I'm going to talk to the judge about getting a writ of habeas corpus."

Steven groaned and held the telephone receiver away from his ear. The last thing he wanted was legal advice from this Cable Guy who wasn't even a cable guy. Right now, he needed someone like—not that he watched *way* too much television—Douglas Wambaugh.

"I'll tell you how we win this thing," the

Cable Guy went on confidently. "I've got it all planned out. We'll put the whole system on trial!"

Steven lifted the receiver back to his ear. "Why are you doing this to me?"

"I didn't do this to you, *you* did this to you," the Cable Guy said, shaking his finger sternly. "You need to learn who your friends are."

More accurately, who his friends *weren't*. "You set me up," Steven said quietly. ·

"No, I taught you a lesson," the Cable Guy corrected him. "I can be your best friend, or your worst enemy. You seem to prefer the latter."

Steven glared at him. "I'll never be your friend. You need help."

The Cable Guy flinched as he absorbed that blow, but then he promptly went on the offensive. "Right now, it's you who needs help, Steven," he said, gesturing to indicate the scene around them—as though Steven could *forget* that he was in jail. "I understand if you wish to seek other representation. I'm just here to give you comfort." He put his hand up to the glass. "Come on, touch it."

Steven just stared at him.

"Come on," the Cable Guy said encouragingly. "You need human contact. Touch it."

Could this guy be any more nuts? "I will *not* touch it," Steven answered.

The other prisoners were beginning to stare now, and Steven tried to pretend that he didn't even know who the Cable Guy was. This little scene wasn't exactly going to help him rise in the prison pecking order anytime soon. It might not be necessary to be popular in jail, but it would be nice. He glanced up and saw that the Cable Guy's hand was still pressed up against the glass.

"Stop it!" he ordered, smacking the barrier with his fist. "Stop it!"

The Cable Guy laughed. "I was just messing with your mind," he said jovially. "Remember *Midnight Express? Awesome* film. Oliver Stone won the Academy Award for the screenplay."

The absolute *last* thing Steven felt like discussing right now was various scenes from *Midnight Express.* "Guard!" he yelled. "Guard!"

The guard ignored him.

"Hmmm," the Cable Guy said with a smile. "He doesn't seem to be paying much attention. I guess that free cable I gave him has affected his hearing." Then he winked dangerously at Steven. "There's no place I can't get to you, Steven. I'm in the crawl space of your soul."

"Guard. This is the guy who framed me!" Steven yelled. "Arrest him!"

"Hey, Bernie," the Cable Guy said, and

reached out to shake the guard's hand. "How's that sports package?" He turned back to Steven. "Don't you worry about Robin. I'll make sure she's well taken care of."

Hearing that, Steven lunged furiously at the glass, using both fists to try and break it. "You go near her, I'll kill you!" he yelled.

A guard jumped forward and dragged him away from the glass towards the detention area.

The Cable Guy nodded thoughtfully as he watched him go.

"This concludes our broadcast day," he said, and then pretended to use a remote. "Click!"

The detention area door slammed shut.

# Chapter Twelve

After his goodwill visit to the prison to give Steven comfort and succor, the Cable Guy had promised to meet Robin at an outdoor cafe. He arrived a little early, so he put on his Walkman to kill some time.

Lately, whenever he had a chance, he would listen to the "How to Cure Your Lisp in Thirty Days" tape that Steven had given him. People at adjoining tables looked at him oddly as he spoke aloud along with the tape, but he didn't even really notice them. Besides, he always liked being the center of attention.

"Seashells. Seashells," he recited, carefully over-pronouncing each word. "Salmon. Salmon. Silverware. Silverware. Suspicious.

Suspicious. Sensational. Sensational."

A hostess was bringing Robin over to the table and the Cable Guy quickly turned off the Walkman, lowered his headphones, and stood up to be polite. Then he sat down in perfect sync with her.

Robin smiled at him forlornly. She had dark circles under her eyes, and looked as though she hadn't gotten any sleep the night before. "Hello."

"Hello," he said, echoing her solemnity. "I'm sorry we have to meet under these circumstances."

"Me too," she answered. "Believe me."

He let a respectful silence pass before going on. "I know we don't know each other very well," he started, "but we *do* have one thing in common—our concern for Steven."

"Well, you were right," she said sadly. "Something terrible's happening with him, and he won't even acknowledge it."

The Cable Guy's nod was grave. "If he refuses to admit he has a problem, we may have to let him hit bottom." He shook his head regretfully. "It looks like he's gonna need some tough love."

Robin nodded, then glanced across the table at him. "You know," she started, very tentative. "His lawyer told me that the police said nobody named Ernie Douglas works for the cable company."

The Cable Guy looked startled for a second, but then he chuckled. "Did they do a name search?" he asked, and slapped his knee in amusement. " 'Cause I work always under a pseudonym so the customers won't harass me at home."

Robin looked at him suspiciously.

"I'm sorry, I can understand why you were confused." He put his hand out to introduce himself. "My real name is Larry, Larry Tate."

Robin shook his hand briefly and then extricated her hand when he wouldn't let go right away. "And Steven's also saying he received all the stereo equipment from you."

"I know," the Cable Guy said with a smile that was a model of tolerance and gentility, "and I'm not mad. He's been cornered, so he's telling some wives' tales. He doesn't mean to hurt me."

Robin let out a deep sigh. How could she have let all of this happen to the man she loved? She should have been paying closer attention to him. "I just feel like I triggered this with him," she confessed. "It's not that I don't want to get married, it's just I feel like he wanted to get married just to *get* married, you know?" Then she looked sheepish. "I don't deal well with pressure."

The Cable Guy reached over and covered her hand with his. "Hey, welcome to the human race, my dear," he said kindly. "We're not perfect. Everybody thinks they have to look like a *Baywatch* babe, and have the wit of *Seinfeld*. He has twenty writers!" He glanced around them. "Hope I'm not getting too loud!"

Robin nodded in total agreement with him. He really was deep. "I could really go for some turkey and mashed potatoes right now," she said, as though the confession had purged a great weight from the depths of her soul.

"Comfort food," the Cable Guy said, nodding. "Bring it on!"

"Exactly," Robin agreed, and then she laughed.

"You've got a great laugh," the Cable Guy said sincerely. "Can I make a request? I'd like to hear it a little more often."

Robin blushed. As far as she could tell, the Cable Guy was a little off-beat—but he was not without charm.

In the prison administration area the next afternoon, the television up on the wall was tuned to *Hard Copy*. The anchorman, Barry Nolan, sat behind a desk and gave the latest news update on—what else?—the Sam Sweet trial.

"The Sam Sweet trial has been thrown into chaos as a result of a videotape made a month after the killing," he reported breathlessly. "In this *Hard Copy* exclusive, Sam Sweet puts on a macabre show for his friends at a party. The judge has not decided whether this tape is admissible as evidence."

The camera cut to a shaky videotape that showed Sam Sweet at a party, with the time and date—so it was clearly *after* the murder— seen in the corner of the screen. Sam was standing next to a wall, which was completely covered with a huge mirror. He gestured at his reflection in the mirror.

"Hey, everyone," Sam Sweet said, leering at the video camera. "Look, it's me and—" He gestured towards the mirror—"my brother Stan." He waved mockingly at his reflection. "Hi, Stan. It's so nice to see you. How are you feeling?" He winked at the camera. "Look, he's alive!"

Then, out of nowhere, Sam's expression changed and he punched the mirror, shattering it.

"Now he's *dead*," he said angrily.

Realizing that he had revealed too much, he forced a strained smile.

"What?" he said, apparently to whoever was holding the camera. "Oh, I'm just goofing around."

The camera cut back to Barry Nolan. "The judge has yet to rule on whether or not the tape will be admissible in court. Mr. Sweet's performance may not earn him an Emmy, but it might put him behind bars!" Barry glanced up at the teleprompter. "Next, *Highway Hunks*. Stay with us."

In the prison administration area, a group of police officers was gathered around the television set in total fascination. At the front desk, Steven's father was paying his bail.

Steven stood next to him, his shoulder slumped. "I'm sorry, Dad," he muttered.

Earl frowned at him. "I don't want to hear it. Do you know the pain you put your mother through? You're lucky she isn't dead from this!"

"I didn't do anything," Steven insisted. "You have to believe me."

Earl nodded, not buying that for a second. "Just like you said you didn't steal that *X-Men* comic book when you were eight," he reminded him. "Then I found it in your—"

"Underwear drawer," they both finished at the exact same time.

Hearing the phrase "underwear drawer," all of the police officers looked over curiously, but then returned their attention to the Sam Sweet trial.

Steven sighed, since his father had been bringing that particular episode up constantly for the last twenty years. He had only been eight years old. "Will you ever stop mentioning that?" he asked.

Earl snapped his checkbook shut. "This cost me a lot of money. You jump bail, I swear I'll hire one of those . . ." He paused, trying to think of the right word. ". . . *guys* to hunt you down."

"A bounty hunter?" Steven guessed.

"Exactly," his father said.

Steven sighed. He was going to go straight from *Midnight Express* to *Midnight Run*.

He and his father didn't talk much on the ride over to his apartment. Earl was too angry, and Steven was too tired. His father dropped him off at the curb in front of the building and Steven dragged himself up the stairs to his apartment, exhausted from his jail experience. If he had ever had any doubts in that area, he now knew that he wasn't cut out to be a hardened convict.

When he walked into the living room, he saw several new frames hanging up on the wall. They were four-foot-high blow-ups of Polaroid photographs of Steven with his arm around the Cable Guy at the karaoke jam. The photos had been expensively and stylishly tinted.

Furious, Steven ran to the wall and took all of the photographs down, throwing them into a large pile in the corner of the room.

The Cable Guy was, easily, the most clueless nemesis that had ever been born.

Steven's parents' fortieth anniversary party was that night, and Robin agreed to go with him. So far, they hadn't really discussed the implications of his arrest, but he could tell that she was very disturbed by the whole thing. *He* was too.

Before they went over, Steven looked down at his sweatshirt and jeans and went back to his bedroom to change. He put on his best suit and tie, in the hopes that at least that would please his parents. If he'd had time, he would have gotten a haircut too.

"Are you sure you're okay?" Robin asked as they walked up to his parents' front door.

"Yes," Steven said tightly, although he was dreading this evening. "I'm fine."

She shook her head. "You're not fine. When you say you're fine, I know you're not fine."

All right, so he wasn't fine. In fact, he was lousy. "I just want to get this over with, so I can go home and get some rest," he said.

She nodded sympathetically.

He didn't want to take his bad mood out on

her, so he picked up her hand and gave it a squeeze.

Robin smiled at him and squeezed back. "I want you to know I invited your friend," she said. "He was concerned about you."

Steven nodded, only half-listening as he reached out to ring the doorbell. "Great. I feel bad, I've kind of been blowing Rick off lately."

"Not Rick," Robin said.

The door swung open and, standing there, dressed to kill, was the Cable Guy.

"You can only come in if you came to rage!" he announced cheerfully.

Steven's mouth dropped open in shock. There was no escape. Now the Cable Guy had even infiltrated his family!

Robin smiled and walked past him to the front hall. As Steven started to step forward, the Cable Guy put a hand on his chest to stop him.

"Is this guy cool?" he asked Robin, and then laughed heartily and poked Steven in the ribs. "I'm just joshing, pal. Come on in."

Once they were inside, and the Cable Guy had gone off towards the kitchen, Steven whirled on Robin.

"What is he doing here?" he asked, enraged.

Robin shrugged and took off her coat. "What do you mean? I invited him."

Was he starting to get paranoid, or was the

entire world suddenly turning against him? *"When* did you invite him?" Steven asked.

Robin took a wooden hanger out of the front closet and slipped her coat onto it. "At lunch the other day," she answered as she put her coat away.

"At lunch?" Steven repeated. "You had *lunch* with him?"

The Cable Guy came bounding back out to the foyer to see what was taking them so long.

"Hello," Robin said and gave him a peck on the cheek. "You look great."

Seeing the kiss, Steven winced.

"And *you* are a vision," the Cable Guy told her. "Hello, Steven." He grinned devilishly. "You're looking rested."

Steven grabbed him by the lapels and pulled him aside. "Come here."

The Cable Guy shook free from his grip and then brushed any possible lint or wrinkles from his suit. "Are you okay, Steven?" he asked dryly. "I'm getting some really weird energy from you."

Oh yeah, funny. "Maybe," Steven said through his teeth, "it's because I just got out of prison, where *you* sent me. I should just drag you to the police right now."

"Come on, Steven, let's just have a good time tonight," the Cable Guy said, a crazy gleam in his eye.

Steven's parents and Robin walked over to them with smiles pasted on their faces. It was hard to be sure, but his parents looked as though they were determined to put the best possible spin on things.

"Steven, your mother and I had a long talk with your friend Larry here when he came over earlier to screw in the cable," his father began.

Larry? Steven frowned.

"Thank you again for that," Steven's mother said to the Cable Guy.

The Cable Guy waved that aside, looking shy.

"Anyway, Steven," his father went on. "We owe you an apology. We didn't know what you were going through until he told us."

"We are *so* sorry," his mother added.

Earl nodded. "We just didn't get involved with stuff like that when I was your age."

Steven narrowed his eyes, trying to figure out what kind of lie the Cable Guy had told them. Clearly, some obscure form of addictive behavior was somewhere in the equation.

"I know we haven't been there for you lately, but we're going to see you through this, 'cause we're a *family*," his father promised.

"And . . . ?" the Cable Guy prompted him.

Earl had to think for a second, but then he

nodded. "I love you," he said and gave Steven a big hug.

Steven grimaced. His parents had been *prepped* by the Cable Guy? This was increasingly Kafkaesque. If he weren't so exhausted, it might even seem funny. "Uh, thanks, Dad," he said.

Steven's mother smiled sweetly at the Cable Guy. "You've got a good friend here, Steven."

No, he had a merciless *archenemy*, with deceptively brilliant social skills.

His parents led him into the living room, where the entire family had gathered for pre-dinner cocktails.

Steven's brother Pete came over, carrying a small baby strapped to his chest.

"Hey, buddy," he said with a wink. "We're with you. Keep your chin up."

Steven smiled thinly—and headed straight for the kitchen to pour himself a drink.

At dinner, the Cable Guy monopolized the conversation, and to Steven's amazement, his entire family seemed to be charmed by him. While everyone else talked and laughed and enjoyed their meal, Steven just stared down at his untouched plate and refilled his glass every so often.

"So," the Cable Guy said, launching into yet another story. This one seemed to be about the night they'd spent at Medieval Times. "Steven is carrying this battle ax, and he's chasing me, swinging like a madman. I'm yelling at him, 'Hey, it's just a show! Come on, what are you trying to prove?'"

He just *hated* the Cable Guy. He hated him with every fiber of his being. He hated him with a passion.

"He always takes things too seriously," Steven's little sister was saying.

The Cable Guy nodded. "Tell me something I *don't* know. The guy almost took my head off!"

Everyone laughed, watching the Cable Guy with rapt attention.

Steven just glowered across the table at him, his eyes filled with rage.

For some reason, the Cable Guy was now talking and eating in slow motion, and Steven kept staring at him, getting more and more irritated.

"What are you doing?" he blurted out finally.

The Cable Guy stopped moving in slow-motion. "Remember *Goodfellas*? Martin Scorsese uses slow-motion photography to enhance his chilling tale of four wiseguys," he recited. "I'm Jimmy Two Times." He resumed his slow-motion movements, and Steven's family laughed raucously.

Tony, Steven's six-year-old nephew, ran over to the Cable Guy with a toy gun. "Pow, pow, pow," he yelled, pretending to fire the gun. "You're under arrest."

"A young cop, trying to make a name for himself," the Cable Guy observed dryly.

Everyone laughed, while Steven just shook his head. As far as he was concerned, being arrested wasn't funny at all.

The Cable Guy started running around the table to escape, and Tony chased him, giggling all the way.

"I thought we had an arrangement," the Cable Guy shouted over his shoulder.

Tony stopped and pretended to fire again.

"You'll never catch me, copper!" the Cable Guy vowed.

"Pow, pow, pow!" Tony shouted back, and kept firing his toy gun.

The Cable Guy stopped to grab a green bean from the table. He put it between his lip and nose, pretending that it was a mustache.

"You'll never get me," he vowed. "I'm gonna wear a disguise."

Just then, Steven remembered something. The artist's rendering of the man who had beaten up Robin's date in the restroom flashed into his mind, and he mentally superimposed it onto the Cable Guy's face. With the green bean mustache, he looked totally different, and with growing horror, Steven realized that they were one and the same person.

The Cable Guy kept running, but then he dropped the bean.

"My cover's blown!" he said.

Tony pointed his gun at the Cable Guy and shrieked "Pow!" at the top of his lungs.

Instantly, the Cable Guy crumpled to the floor, grabbing his midsection as though he had been shot. "Oh, you got me, just when I was gonna go legit," he moaned, then played dead.

Tony swaggered over to check the corpse. When he got close enough, the Cable Guy unexpectedly lunged up to grab him around the waist.

"Aaaah!" he screamed in a crazed voice. "Nobody messes with me and lives!"

Tony laughed hysterically, squirmed free, and raced out of the room. The Cable Guy scrambled to his feet and chased after him.

Fearing for Tony's safety, Steven jumped up from the table to follow them.

"Isn't that nice?" Earl said to the rest of the family. "Steven's finally getting in the spirit of things."

By the time Steven got out to the hallway, they were nowhere in sight. If anything happened to Tony, he would never forgive himself.

He ran around the house, looking for his nephew, frantic with worry. He was in the library when suddenly, from behind a couch, Tony and the Cable Guy popped out.

"Boo!" they shouted.

Steven flew back, scared out of his wits. "Yow!" he cried out.

Tony and the Cable Guy just laughed their heads off. They were both having a grand old time, enjoying the success of their little prank.

"Oh man, you should have seen your face," the Cable Guy said, wiping away tears of laughter. "It was *classic*."

"Very funny," Steven said without cracking a smile. "Tony, go to your mother!"

Tony immediately started crying and ran out of the room.

"Look what you've done," the Cable Guy said, trying to sound disgusted, but still chuckling a little.

"I know you beat up Robin's date," Steven said.

The Cable Guy's laughter stopped on a dime and he returned Steven's scowl. "Well, I guess I did what you didn't have the *guts* to do," he answered.

"You stay away from Robin," Steven warned him.

The Cable Guy's expression faded into the dark and deeply disturbed look Steven had only seen once before. "Don't mess with me," he said, his voice so furious that it was almost unrecognizable. "I'm feeling like a part of the family, and I *like* it." He paused. "You should try it some time."

Before Steven could respond, his mother came into the room. She looked at the two of them, and then shook her head. "My, you two look like brothers," she said. "Come on back, we're all having coffee in the living room."

The Cable Guy's expression changed so swiftly back to a benign and nonthreatening smile that, for a second, Steven thought he might have imagined the sinister one.

The Cable Guy went over to the doorway and took Steven's mother's arm. "Are you guys trying to fatten me up?" he asked happily. " 'Cause if you are, you're doing a really good job of it."

As the two of them laughed together and walked out of the room, Steven stayed where he was for a minute, his features knotted with worry.

His family was dealing with a total psychopath here, and they didn't even seem to realize it.

# Chapter Thirteen

When he finally went out to the living room, everyone was already halfway through dessert. Steven had long since lost his appetite, so he just shook his head when they offered him a piece of chocolate cheesecake.

After finishing dessert, they all lingered over their coffee. Everyone was laughing as the Cable Guy told joke after joke. Everyone seemed to *love* the Cable Guy. Steven was mortified. Had his entire family lost their minds in one fell swoop? Or had they vacationed in Stepford recently, and no one had remembered to tell him?

Robin saw that Steven was looking upset.

"Come on, Steven, relax," she said. "We're just having fun."

Some fun. He'd rather have his leg amputated than see his enemy so . . . *loved*. He stood up abruptly. "No, I've had enough," he said. "I can't do this. I won't sit here with *him*."

His father got up too, with his usual stern look. "Steven, I really think you're over-reacting."

"I am *not* overreacting," Steven retorted. "You're all being fooled! He's not like this!"

"Let's all relax," the Cable Guy said softly to the rest of the family. "We knew this was going to happen."

Who did this guy think he was!? "Nothing is happening!" Steven shouted.

The Cable Guy reached out and put his hand on his arm. "Steven, this is a safe place," he promised. "You're with people who love you. Right, everyone?"

"Yes, we love you," Steven's family and Robin all chanted in unison. "We love you."

This was just too much. "I hate you!" Steven screamed at the Cable Guy. "Get out of my life!"

Unfazed, the Cable Guy just shrugged helplessly at the others. "He's projecting all his anger onto me. Maybe I should go."

"No, please don't go," Robin said and

glared at Steven. "Steven, you're being a total jerk."

Earl nodded. "You *had* to ruin our anniversary, didn't you?"

They were all insane. He was the only sane person in the house. "What?" Steven asked, bewildered. This was turning into *Gaslight II*. "What are you talking about?"

"It's okay," the Cable Guy assured everyone. "He's hitting bottom right now." He took both of Steven's arms and looked at him with compassion. "We're here for you."

Steven knocked his hands violently away. "Don't come near me!"

"Now's where the healing begins," the Cable Guy told the family and then leaned closer to Steven so that no one else would hear what he was going to say. "I think I'm in love with Robin."

Steven hauled off and punched him in the face.

The Cable Guy stumbled back a few steps and Robin ran over to help him. As he sagged down, she held him in her arms and looked at Steven bitterly.

"I can't *believe* you," she said.

The Cable Guy regained his balance and stood up. "I'm fine," he said bravely. "Thank you for a delightful evening." He started for the front door, and then paused to give Steven a beneficent smile. "I forgive you."

As he walked piously out of the room, everyone else glared at Steven, blaming him for ruining their lovely, festive evening.

"Well," his mother said finally. "I hope you're happy."

Steven sighed. Oh, yeah he was just *thrilled*.

Picking up the very minor slack where his family had left off, Robin kept yelling at him all the way out to the car when they finally left. For the most part, he tried to tune her out, although he made a point of nodding every so often so she would think he was taking all of it in.

"I just think you were completely out of line," she raged. "I don't know what's happening to you these days."

Fed up, Steven stopped walking long enough to stare at her. "Robin, the guy is a sociopath," he said intensely. "He leaves messages on my machine night and day. He shows up wherever I go. He won't leave me alone."

"*That* sounds familiar," Robin said, and looked at him pointedly.

Steven decided to let that one pass. "You know, he was the one who beat up your date at that restaurant," he told her. "That's right, it was him. And *he* gave you the free cable. It wasn't me."

Robin looked hurt. "But you took the credit for it?"

"Well—" Steven realized that he maybe should have thought first before sharing that particular thing. "That's what he wanted. He was manipulating me." He smiled with relief. "It feels so good to be honest about this."

"Oh come on," Robin said incredulously. "Manipulating you? Don't be ridiculous."

"This is not the point," Steven said hastily. "The point is that this guy has been setting me up. He's responsi—"

She cut him off. "I don't want to hear it. You have some serious problems, and it's not my responsibility to help you. I am only responsible for my own happiness."

Since when? "Where did that come from?" Steven wanted to know.

"It was Jerry Springer's Final Thought," she said and strode down the street without looking back.

Wanting to salvage at least one of the relationships in his life, Steven went over to the television station to try and find Rick. The security people sent him down to the newsroom, and as he walked in, he saw Rick racing off to an editing bay to cut a story together before the eleven o'clock news.

"Hi," Steven ventured. "I—"

"Busy," Rick said briefly as he hurried past. "Can't talk."

Steven decided to follow him anyway. "Look," he said. "I'm sorry I've been blowing you off."

"You better believe you've been blowing me off," Rick agreed.

Steven sighed. "I know. It's just, this guy is really doing a number on me."

Rick squinted at the news footage on the video monitor and pressed a couple of buttons to create some jump cuts. "Hey, I told you not to hang out with him," he said as he rewound and scanned the results of his editing.

"You're the one who told me to offer him money so I could get free cable," Steven pointed out.

Rick shrugged and changed one of his jump cuts to a dissolve. "You didn't tell me he was a psychopath," he said, and then he looked over. "If you want, I'll see if I can get my friend in Research to track him down."

Steven nodded. "Thanks, that would be great," he said. One of the best things about Rick was that he was not only loyal but also pretty forgiving. "His name is Ernie Douglas. His friends call him Chip."

Hearing the name, Rick paused long enough in his editing to frown briefly. "Ernie Douglas?" he asked, thinking aloud. "Ernie Douglas? Why does that sound so *familiar*?"

Steven was dreading the idea of going back to work again, after his unceremonious exit in handcuffs, but since he had bills to pay, he didn't have much choice. To make matters worse, he overslept, and in his rush to get out of the apartment, managed to select a shirt that was missing a button and also to spill coffee on his tie.

When he got to the office, his secretary was watching a news report about the Sam Sweet trial on a mini-television. On the screen, a female prosecutor was gesturing emphatically with a shotgun as she questioned a police officer on the witness stand.

Joan changed channels, and Larry King appeared, interviewing Alan Dershowitz about "the abuse excuse," which Alan seemed to feel was the rankest form of hogwash, and he kept holding up one of his latest books to illustrate the lengthy points he was making.

"Did anyone notice I'm late?" Steven asked, trying to catch his breath.

"What are you talking about," Joan said without looking up, "you've been here for an hour."

Joan was like an angel sometimes. "Thank you," Steven said gratefully, and escaped into his office.

For some reason, his computer was on. He was sure that he had turned it off the last time he was in here, and it seemed strange that the screen saver was flashing, as if applications were still running endlessly. Could Joan have come in here to check one of his files, maybe? Except that she had her own computer, so she would have no reason to use his.

Frowning, Steven clicked a button and a message flashed onto the monitor. It read: "GOOD MORNING, STEVEN. HAVE A WONDERFUL DAY. HERE'S AN EXTRA SPECIAL SURPRISE."

Then an image came onto the screen. It was a black-and-white surveillance video, digitized for the computer. He recognized his own apartment, and saw that it was a film of him talking to Robin, right before they had watched *Sleepless in Seattle* that time.

"Work's good," he was saying.

"How's Hal?" Robin asked.

Steven cringed as he saw himself instantly look animated in response to her question.

"Don't get me started," he was answering. "That guy has no vision. It's like working for Mr. Magoo. And those hair plugs. Does he think nobody notices?"

"It's just great that he approved your project," Robin said.

"I know," he agreed, and then Steven saw

himself chuckle. "Now if only someone at Corporate would smarten up enough to dump *Hal*, I could really get some stuff done."

There was a whir of rewinding, and the scene started again, indicating that it was on a continuous loop.

Steven stared at the screen, aghast. How could this have happened? He looked out into the hall and saw that the scene was playing on every computer in the office.

Was Hal seeing this? Oh no. Panic-stricken, he ran out of his office to try and prevent him from getting anywhere near a computer until he could figure out how to shut the video loop off.

He raced through the office bullpen to the edge of the stairs. The executive offices were on the next floor down, and he could see Hal walking into his office.

Steven tore down the stairs, moving so fast that his feet barely touched the floor, but it was too late. Hal was already sitting behind his desk and staring sadly at his computer screen.

"Think I hate him, hate him, hate him, hate him," Steven's voice was saying on the computer, the echo reverberating through the room.

Hal looked up and saw him standing, looking guilt-ridden, in the doorway.

"I'm *so* sorry," Steven said.

Hal did his best to smile at him, although his lower lip quivered a little. "Don't worry," he said softly. "It's okay, Steven."

But from his stricken expression, Steven knew that it wasn't okay at all.

Steven wasn't surprised when he was fired within the hour, and told to vacate the premises immediately. If he'd had *any* idea that Hal would ever have heard him say those things, he would never have—but, well, it was too late now.

The only person he said good-bye to was Joan, and then he carried a cardboard box filled with his belongings down to the parking garage.

He was walking towards his car, when a nearby car alarm beeped and its headlights flashed. Suddenly, another alarm went off, and then another, and another, until he was surrounded by screaming car alarms and crazily flashing headlights.

"Chip!" he shouted, trying not to sound as terrified as he felt. "Chip, this isn't funny! Where are you?!"

Just then, all of the alarms stopped simultaneously, and the only sound was a maniacal laugh echoing through the parking garage.

Steven ran to his car, threw the door open,

and climbed inside. He tossed his cardboard box unceremoniously into the back seat and locked all of the doors. His hand was shaking so much that he had trouble turning the ignition key, but he finally got the car started and drove up the ramp in a total panic.

From out of nowhere, the Cable Guy stepped from the shadows and into the beam of his headlights. Steven was going so fast that he couldn't stop in time. He screamed and pressed both feet against the brakes, but the car rammed into him with a dull thud.

The Cable Guy was thrown into the air and Steven heard his body land on the roof of the car. Before he fell off, he grabbed onto the bar of the luggage rack and maintained a precarious grip.

Steven looked into his rearview mirror and saw the Cable Guy staring through the back window at him. He yelped in fear, and stepped on the accelerator.

As Steven kept driving, the Cable Guy climbed athletically back onto the roof of the car, using the luggage rack to pull himself up.

"Nothing can stop the Terminator 1000 series," the Cable Guy said in a deep voice. Then he jumped down onto the hood and scrutinized Steven through the windshield with an insane grin on his face.

Steven was so startled that he swerved

wildly and almost lost control of the car as it fishtailed in response. "Leave me alone!" Steven yelled desperately through the windshield. "I have no job, no girlfriend, no family anymore! It's over! You won!"

"Oh no," the Cable Guy answered menacingly. "It's not over." He let out a loud, gleeful cackle. "It's just getting started!"

Steven veered around a sharp corner and the momentum tossed the Cable Guy off his car. The Cable Guy fell onto the cement, rolling many times. Then he used the momentum of the roll to leap to his feet and he ran off into the shadows, scampering like a supernatural bug.

If Steven hadn't been freaked out before, he sure was *now*!

# Chapter Fourteen

As usual, Rick was working late that night at the newsroom. The fast-paced schedule didn't give him much free time lately, but he was picking up a lot of overtime hours, so it was worth it.

He sat at his desk, going through tapes and half-watching the early evening edition of the news. The station's anchorman, Mark Thompson, was reading a story about the ever-popular Sam Sweet trial.

"The jury has notified the judge that they are very close to reaching a verdict and that they would like to keep deliberating into the evening hours," Mark Thompson said into the camera.

"He's guilty," Rick said to the screen. "You know it, Mark, they know it, we all know it."

A female researcher walked over and sat in the padded chair next to his desk. She was the friend he had asked to try and track down the Cable Guy.

"Find anything?" he asked.

She shook her head as she scanned her voluminous notes on the subject of the mysterious and elusive Cable Guy. "There are five people named Ernie Douglas in this county," she said. "Two of them are African-American. One is eighty-five years old. One is only eleven years old, and the last one is in a wheelchair."

Rick sighed. "So we're nowhere."

"I'm afraid so," the researcher agreed. "I did my best. Sorry."

"Ernie Douglas," Rick mused aloud, trying to remember why he knew that name. Somewhere it rang a bell, but he just couldn't put his finger on it. "Ernie Douglas."

The researcher started tapping her foot nervously in a distinct, repetitive rhythm.

"Could you stop that?" he asked.

"Don't snap at me," she answered. "I'm doing this as a favor, remember?"

Rick continued staring at her two-toned, wing-tipped-style shoe, and had a sudden epiphany. "Hey, wait a minute, could you start that again?" he asked eagerly. "Start tapping your foot again!"

She looked confused. "But wait, I thought you just told me to—"

"Humor me," he said.

She rolled her eyes and began tapping her foot again in the same rhythm.

Rick watched her foot move and then whistled a single note, followed by a few more. Before long, he was whistling the theme to *My Three Sons.*

Catching on, she joined in, and they sang more loudly to celebrate breaking the code.

"Nice work," Rick said, grinning at her.

She grinned back. "Don't mention it."

Steven was on his way into his apartment when he heard the telephone ringing. He finished unlocking the door as fast as he could and raced inside to try and answer it before the person on the other end hung up.

"Hello," he panted.

"Bingo," Rick said triumphantly. "*My Three Sons.*"

Of course. How could he have been so stupid? Steven nodded and let his grocery bag drop onto the kitchen table. "Chip and Ernie Douglas," he remembered.

"You got it," Rick said and glanced at the fresh sheaf of notes the researcher had just handed him. "Okay. I've got a list of every cable installer fired in the last four years. Every one of these guys has the same physical description as our friend."

Steven shook his head. So apparently, the guy had been forcing unwanted friendships on people for years. He was a menace, plain and simple.

Rick squinted to read the researcher's handwriting. "Let's see what we have here. Murray Slaughter, Brandon Walsh, Sam Malone, Alex Reiger. There was even"—He glanced at the researcher for confirmation, and she nodded—"a guy who liked to be called 'the Big Ragu?'"

The Cable Guy might be crazy, but at least he was consistent. "Yeah, that was Carmine from *Laverne and Shirley*," Steven said, as he carried his portable phone around the apartment and searched for the Cable Guy's hidden video surveillance camera.

"That's *so* sad that you know that," Rick answered. "Anyway, the cable company in town fired a guy six months ago named Darren Stevens. His boss was Larry Tate, from a little show called *Bewitched*. Get the pattern?"

Just then, Steven located a small, high-tech camera under the coffee table. He scowled and ripped it out.

"So, he doesn't even work for the cable company?" he asked, as he tried to crush the camera in his free hand. No one was ever going to take another surveillance tape of *him*.

Rick checked the researcher's notes. "Yahtzee!" he said triumphantly. "They booted him out for stalking customers. The guy is *deeply* troubled. If I were you, I'd lock up tight."

Oh. Good idea. Steven rushed over to throw the dead bolt on the door and then started locking all of the windows.

"I'll talk to you later," Rick said. "The ball's in your court now!"

Words to live by. "Thanks," Steven answered.

After checking to make sure the apartment was secure, Steven decided that he should try and stay awake, just in case. If the Cable Guy came bursting in, he didn't want to be taken by surprise.

He watched the Weather Channel for a while, struggling to keep his eyes open as a weatherman predicted upcoming "intermittent thunderstorms." It seemed like it never stopped raining these days. The concept of that made him feel even more tired, so he switched over to Court TV, where the defense attorney in the Sam Sweet trial was being interviewed.

Steven was so exhausted that the defense attorney's words sounded more like gibberish. Unless of course it was gibberish. He fell asleep on his bed, still holding the remote control.

Within moments, he was in the middle of a murky and upsetting dream. The defense attorney was there, and his gibberish turned into clearly spoken words. Only this time, the voice sounded more familiar.

In the dream, the television was on and showing the Sam Sweet trial. A prosecutor was in the middle of a passionate final summation—only it was actually the Cable Guy.

"This man killed his own brother," the Cable Guy told the jury. "Some people don't even have a brother." He turned to look right into the camera. "Do they, *Steven*? Are you listening to me, Steven? Don't shut it off. Don't shut it—"

In the dream, Steven saw his own hand moving very slowly to turn off the television. He got out of bed and walked down the hallway. For some reason, his entire apartment seemed to be much larger and the walls and corners were all slightly off-kilter.

He looked into the living room and saw Rick standing there, glowering at him.

"Why do you keep blowing me off, man?" the dream-Rick wanted to know, his fists clenched tightly.

Steven kept walking until he came to an elongated version of his bathroom. He opened the door to peek inside. The shower was running and hot steam billowed out at him. For some reason, the two eight-year-old Sweet twins were there, looking very spooky.

Steven shuddered and used all of his weight to shut the door and keep them away. He continued down the long hallway and opened the door to the dining room, except that Robin's bedroom was there, instead.

Robin was in bed, and a man wearing a cable installer's uniform was smothering her with a pillow. Steven lunged forward to help, but the man turned and Steven saw that it was an exact replica of himself, smothering Robin.

Someone was pounding on the front door now and he ran to open it, but nobody was there. Then the Cable Guy popped out of nowhere, holding a cut cable cord.

"You owe me!" he shouted.

Steven slammed the door shut and looked through the peephole to see if he was still out there.

The Cable Guy began to run full-speed at the door. As he did, he got bigger and bigger, and his body became more distorted. He hit the door with a BANG! and stumbled back from the force of the collision. Then he picked himself up, walked to the end of the hall, and ran towards the door even faster. There was another BANG! and the Cable Guy staggered back into position to try again.

Realizing that the door wouldn't hold much longer, Steven tried to run away just as the Cable Guy smashed through it in a spray of splinters and came after him.

Steven ran and ran down his hallway, which appeared to be a mile long. No matter how fast he ran, he didn't seem to make any progress. Every time he looked over his shoulder, he saw the Cable Guy racing after him at an alarming rate of speed, grunting like a wolf.

"I just want to hang out," the Cable Guy said breathlessly. "No big deal."

Steven kept running, and the hallway started getting smaller and smaller, until he had to crawl on the floor to squeeze through it.

Then, suddenly, he reached the end of the hallway and saw that he was trapped. He looked behind him, but the Cable Guy was gone. Steven started back down the hallway, so scared that his legs were shaking.

He found himself back in the very tall living room. The television was still blaring and he sat down on the edge of the couch, not sure what else to do. His conscious brain wanted to wake up, but his subconscious mind had taken over. Overwhelmed by the nightmare, he put his head in his hands.

When he looked up, he saw the Cable Guy's

face on the television set. The face stretched out from the television, growing larger, and larger, and larger still.

"Steven, you're just like me," the Cable Guy told him insidiously. "We're cut from the same cloth. We're one and the same!"

Then the face opened its mouth and swallowed Steven, pulling him into the television.

At that point, Steven woke up and found himself sitting straight up in bed, trembling uncontrollably, his body drenched in a cold sweat.

"I am not a smotherer!" he gasped, not sure where he was or how he had gotten there.

The telephone rang, and he snatched it off the hook.

"I am not a smotherer!" he shouted.

"Who said you were?" the Cable Guy's voice asked matter-of-factly.

Okay, *this* wasn't a dream anymore; this was real. "Oh no," Steven groaned. His life had become a total nightmare whether he was awake or not.

"It didn't have to come to this, Steven," the Cable Guy said, sounding both fierce and sad. "We could have been blood brothers."

Perish the thought. "Rick told me you were fired from the cable company," Steven answered. "You're not even a real cable guy."

There was a long, ugly silence.

"Do you feel good now that you've hurt me?" the Cable Guy asked, his voice breaking slightly.

"Look." Steven took a deep breath, wanting to seem very calm. "Let's just—"

"Well, now I'm going to have to hurt you," the Cable Guy went on without missing a beat. "I'm going to take away what you hold dearest in the world."

Robin! Steven clenched his fist around the telephone receiver. "I swear, if you touch—"

"Could you hold on a second, I've got call waiting," the Cable Guy interrupted him. "It'll just be a second."

Steven heard a click, and then he was put on hold. What kind of wacko used call waiting at a time like this? And where was he? Sitting someplace in his van? Parked outside this very apartment building?

Steven sat stiffly on the side of his bed, gripping the phone, afraid to hang up or even move. Right this moment, Robin might be in mortal danger, and if he hung up, he would never be able to find her. A minute passed, and then another, and soon, he had been on hold for about five minutes.

Then the Cable Guy clicked back. "Sorry about that," he said. "Where was I?" He thought. "Oh yeah. You're going to feel my wrath."

"Don't do this," Steven pleaded. "There must be some way for us to work this out."

The Cable Guy, who was crouching in the musty air duct above Robin's bedroom closet and speaking over a cellular phone, sighed heavily. A daddy longlegs spider scuttled across his face, but he didn't even notice that it was there.

"I wish there was," he answered dully. Then he sighed again, starting to lose it. "Oh, Steven, I'm just so tired. So very tired."

Okay, vulnerability was good. He would *work* with vulnerability. "Let's talk in person, okay?" Steven suggested. "Where are you?"

"Well, I'd love to chat," the Cable Guy said, and then burst into insane peals of laughter, "but I've got a date with a very charming young lady." He paused. "You might know her. I think you guys went out at one point." He paused again, and then chuckled softly. "Her name is Robin."

"Stay away from her!" Steven warned him. "Or I swear I'll—"

"Good-bye, Steven," the Cable Guy whispered, then hung up.

Steven listened to the dial tone for a few seconds, his heart pounding with fear. Then he threw the telephone across the room, yanked on a pair of jeans, and jumped into his sneakers. He grabbed his car keys and his wallet, and raced outside to his car.

Robin was in trouble, and he was the only one who could save her!

# Chapter Fifteen

It was pitch-dark outside and a light drizzle was falling. The streets were still slick from when it had rained earlier that day, and Steven's tires fought for traction as he steered the car out of the parking lot and out onto the main boulevard, pressing the accelerator all the way to the floor.

He sped through the quiet city, running red lights and stop signs in his rush to get to Robin's apartment. There was almost no traffic, and he tore up hills and swerved around corners in a race against time—and a man who was clearly in the middle of a full-fledged, cable-ready, psychotic breakdown.

Finally, he saw her building up ahead. He

screeched to a stop in the middle of the street and leaped out of the car, leaving the door open and the engine running. He dashed up to Robin's apartment door and rang her bell.

"Robin!" he shouted, and then pounded on the door. "Robin!"

Hearing the noise, one of Robin's neighbors came out onto the balcony.

"Take it easy, okay? She just left with the man from the cable company," she said.

Steven felt his heart sink. "Do you know where they were going?"

The neighbor shrugged and flipped ahead to the television section. "Oh, I don't know," she said, as she ran a finger down the listings for that night's programs. "But he said they were taking a ride on the information super-highway."

Lightning flashed in the sky, and Steven's eyes widened in fright. At least now he knew where they were heading, but would he be able to get there in time? He still wasn't sure what the Cable Guy was planning to do, but he knew that it wouldn't be pretty.

There was a loud clap of thunder, and then it began to rain hard. Steven ran back to his car through the downpour, ducking instinctively as lightning flashed less than a block away.

Somehow, he had to get to the satellite dish before it was too late.

Lightning crackled in the sky and thunder rumbled in the distance as the Cable Guy gave Robin the same tour he had given Steven of the satellite dish that sat so majestically above the city, bringing hours of wonderful programming to millions of contented viewers.

"It all started in Lansford, Pennsylvania, where Panther Valley Television, with the assistance of Jerrod Electronics, created the first cable television system," he told her proudly, as they looked up at the gigantic dish.

Robin wasn't sure why she had agreed to come along with the Cable Guy, but he had insisted that he had important news about Steven and that they needed to discuss it someplace private. Now that they were together, though, his eyes seemed wild and unfocused, and she wished that she had stayed home, where it was warm and dry.

The Cable Guy took her hand to lead her up to the edge of the dish, and she followed him reluctantly.

"Careful now," he advised. "Gets mighty slippery."

Robin nodded, struggling to keep her footing on the muddy slope. Where was Steven anyway? Wasn't he supposed to be meeting them here?

"The future is now," the Cable Guy proclaimed, once they had reached the top of the dish. "Soon, every American home will integrate their television, phone, and computer. You'll be able to visit the Louvre on one channel and watch American Gladiators on another."

Robin nodded and looked around uneasily. The whole area seemed too quiet, and the fierce storm made everything appear all the more isolated and frightening.

"You can do your shopping at home," the Cable Guy enthused, lost in the rhapsody that was television. "Or play a game of Mortal Kombat with a friend in Vietnam."

"This is, uh, really fascinating," Robin said politely. "But I really think we ought to go now."

The Cable Guy gave her a wide, unbalanced smile. "I knew you'd appreciate it, Robin," he answered warmly. "I brought Steven here once, but it turned out he didn't care about my interests."

It was raining even harder now, and Robin couldn't help shivering. She had forgotten to bring a jacket, so she wrapped her arms around herself instead. "Well, I've enjoyed seeing all of this, but we really should go. I'm worried about Steven," she said.

"Steven, Steven, Steven," the Cable Guy repeated grimly. "What is this? A *feast* of Steven?" He showed his teeth in a threatening smile. "Maybe Steven should be worried about *you*." Then he frowned. "Now, what was I trying to say? Stop interrupting."

Understanding for the first time that she was in serious danger, Robin gulped.

The Cable Guy blinked rapidly, and shook his head to clear it. "So. Where was I?"

"Any place you want to be," she assured him, not wanting to make a bad situation any worse.

"You don't know how right you are," he said.

By now, the rain was coming down so hard that it was practically a monsoon. Lightning flashed in every direction, and Steven had to keep swerving to avoid fallen tree branches as he drove up the muddy dirt road to the satellite dish.

Halfway up the hill, his car got stuck in the mud. He pressed down on the accelerator and rocked the steering wheel from side to side, trying to get free, but the back wheels just spun in place.

Steven punched the steering wheel in frustration. This was the last thing he needed.

He got out of the car and ran the rest of the way up the hill to the chain-link fence that surrounded the satellite dish. It was hard to see in the driving rain, and he had to keep rubbing his soggy shirtsleeve across his eyes to clear his vision.

Then he heard the sound of horse hooves coming towards him and he whirled around to try and locate them. The pounding hooves came closer and closer, heading away from the satellite dish, until he saw a headless man on a horse galloping at top speed straight towards the fence.

The horse had on the coat of arms from the Medieval Times restaurant, and Steven groaned. It was clear now; he was doomed to keep living in the middle of this bad dream for the rest of his life. With his luck, there were probably a bunch of serfs and screaming tourists nearby too.

When the horse was almost near the fence, the headless horseman used his sword to smash through the heavy chain and padlock securing the fence. The gate flew open and the headless horseman and his horse rode through it.

The horse raced full-speed directly at Steven, who was forced to jump out of the way so that he wouldn't be trampled. He landed in the mud on all fours, his heart thudding against his chest.

The headless horseman reined the horse to a stop, and the horse reared up on its hind legs, whinnying shrilly. The rider brought him under control, and then the Cable Guy popped his head up through the top of the headless horseman's long black coat.

"Ichabod Crane!" he announced. "The Disney Channel showed it all last month!"

Television. Once again, it always came down to television. Steven staggered to his feet and tried to wipe the mud from his clothes.

The Cable Guy shrugged a few times until the coat had settled comfortably around his shoulders. Then he slapped the reins against the horse's neck, gave him a light kick in the side, and cantered towards Steven again.

"Last time we fought, I let you win!" he shouted, his voice fading in and out of the wind. "Not this time!" Then he imitated the famous Las Vegas announcer, who acted as a commentator for so many sporting events on pay-per-view. "Let's get ready to ruuuuummmmbbbble!"

Steven tried to dodge out of the way, but the Cable Guy leaped off his horse and landed right on top of him. They both slammed into a puddle of mud, trying to get their hands free so they could strangle each other.

Steven got a good shot in with his right elbow, and the Cable Guy fell back for a second. Taking advantage of the momentary weakness, Steven rolled on top of him.

"Where's Robin?!" he shouted, shaking the Cable Guy as hard as he could.

"This isn't about Robin," the Cable Guy screamed back, as they struggled furiously in the rain. "This is about you and me!"

They were both covered with mud like ancient warriors from the rain forest. The Cable Guy lunged up to bite Steven's hand, his teeth sinking in powerfully. Steven winced and punched him in the face with his free hand.

"Where's Robin??" he bellowed.

The Cable Guy responded with an unexpectedly sweet and guileless smile. "I'm sorry," he said. "I didn't catch the question?"

The guy was totally, completely, absolutely, and in every way, *loony tunes*.

While Steven was staring down at him, utterly speechless, the Cable Guy's legs flew up around his neck in a crab hold. He used the momentum to turn the tables and flip back on top of Steven.

Steven, now flat on his back in the mud, used his hands to box the Cable Guy's ears savagely. The Cable Guy let out a little squeal of pain and flew backwards.

Now Steven was on top again, and he fumbled frantically in the mud until his grasping fingers found a large rock. He slammed it down as hard as he could, but the Cable Guy was able to angle his body so that the rock just missed the side of his head.

The rock landed harmlessly in the mud, and they both stared at it for a second.

The Cable Guy was the first one to break the panting silence. "Yes, Luke," he said in a deep, Darth Vader voice. "Give in to the Dark Side of the Force."

Shocked by his own violence, Steven lost his concentration, and the Cable Guy jumped back on top of him. He smiled toothily and then pulled a portable drill from his tool belt.

"I think," he said, with a lilt of melodious menace in his voice, as he turned the drill on, "it's time to make you cable ready." He pursed his lips thoughtfully as he looked down.

Slowly, he brought the spinning drill down towards Steven's face. Steven was both mesmerized and terrified by the sight. Then he reached blindly behind him until his hand found a large tree branch.

He closed his hand around the end of the branch and used it to bat the Cable Guy away from him, striking him across the face with it.

The Cable Guy overreacted, staggering

around in the mud and holding his face like Quasimodo.

"You treat me like the TV!" he rambled crazily. "You use me, but you can't live without me! You can't shut me off with your remote control! I'm not like Robin and Rick and Mommy and Daddy and brother and sister and cousin—"

Remembering the roundhouse battle ax move the Cable Guy had used during their fight at Medieval Times, Steven used both hands to swing his branch and upended the Cable Guy. The Cable Guy's feet went out from under him, and he fell to the ground, unconscious.

Steven looked down at his limp body, and then let the branch fall from his trembling hands. "I got the point," he said.

Unsurprisingly, the comatose Cable Guy had no response to that.

"Steven!" Robin called feebly from someplace off in the distance.

Steven peered up at the outline of the satellite dish through the sheets of rain, but he couldn't see her. She had to be up there somewhere. He ran through the open gate and scaled the muddy slope to the top of the dish, slipping and sliding every step of the way.

When he finally reached the top, he hoisted himself up and climbed over the edge of the satellite dish. Below him, he saw that the bottom of the dish was filled with several feet of filthy rainwater.

Three wires snaked out from the points on the edge of the dish and met at a point in the center of the satellite, thirty feet above the floor of the dish. Robin was hanging by her bound wrists from the center of where those wires met.

Steven gasped, and scrambled down towards the bottom of the dish to try and rescue her.

"Help me, Steven!" she begged, sounding close to tears.

Below them, the Cable Guy had lurched to his feet and was now climbing unsteadily through an entry hatch at the top of the dish.

Seeing the approaching figure, Robin's eyes filled with terror.

"Steven! Look out!" she warned him, as she swung perilously from the wires.

"Yeah, Steven," the Cable Guy sneered, and then mimicked her voice. "Look out!"

Then he sprang out of the hatch like a jack-in-the-box. He slid smoothly down the side of the dish with both feet raised. Steven looked up just as the Cable Guy slammed right into him and knocked him down.

They tumbled down the slope of the dish and rolled all the way into the water. They both sank from sight and then bobbed up to the surface, gasping for air.

"I've missed you," the Cable Guy chirped, and then demurely batted his eyes.

Steven just stared at him, as they both kept treading water.

The Cable Guy grabbed Steven's hair and started dunking his head in and out of the water. He kept doing it until he got bored, and then pulled him up high enough to look straight into his face.

" 'Dry land is not a myth, I've seen it,' " he recited dramatically.

Steven coughed and choked, trying to clear the water from his lungs.

"Kevin Costner, from *Waterworld*," the Cable Guy elaborated. "I don't know what the fuss was about, that movie *ruled*. I saw it six times."

Well, both times Steven saw it, *he* thought it stank.

The Cable Guy pulled him under the water, then yanked him back up. "Isn't it weird that we've wound up in this position?" he asked and shoved him under again.

Steven fought his way back to the surface, where he gasped for air.

"I mean, who would of thunk it?" the Cable Guy asked rhetorically.

Steven gathered all of his strength and

punched him in the mouth with such tremendous force that the blow appeared to knock his
jaw out of alignment.

"You're going to have to do better than *that*,
Steven," the Cable Guy said with no lisp whatsoever. Then he looked startled. "Steven," he
said again, overemphasizing the *S* and realizing that his lisp was magically gone. "Hey, my
lisp is gone!"

Steven hit him again, this time on the other
side of his face.

"You stupid idiot," the Cable Guy swore,
his lisp back.

Ferociously glad that the lisp had returned,
Steven head-butted the Cable Guy as hard as
he could. The Cable Guy's eyes rolled back in
his head, his body went limp, and then he
slipped under the water, unconscious. Then,
very gradually, he sank out of sight.

It was over.

# Chapter Sixteen

"**S**teven!" Robin cried helplessly, still hanging suspended from the three wires by her wrists.

Steven swam with strong strokes to the side of the dish, and then climbed up to the top. There was a rope attached to a pulley, and he swiftly untied the two tight square knots holding the whole thing together.

When he finally loosened the knots, he gently lowered Robin down to the safety of the dish. Once she had landed on her feet, he dropped the rope and ran over to untie her wrists just as the rain gradually began to taper off.

After Robin had been untied, the two of

them sat in the dish, a few feet away from the edge of the water. It had stopped raining completely by now, but they were both soaked as well as exhausted from their ordeal.

They sat without speaking, content just to hold each other close.

"I'm sorry I didn't believe you about him," Robin said softly. "I love you."

"I love you too," Steven whispered back. "And you're right. We shouldn't get married."

Neither of them noticed the Cable Guy's nose slowly break the surface of the water and start sucking in lungfuls of life-giving air.

"I know I've got a lot of problems to work out," Steven said with complete honesty, "which have absolutely nothing to do with you."

Robin smiled at him and hugged him closer. "Don't worry. We'll work them out together," she said.

They were kissing when Steven thought he felt a wet hand fasten around his ankle. He looked down and saw that he was being dragged back into the water by the inexplicably alive Cable Guy.

"Steven, Steven!" Robin shouted as she tried to pull him free.

"Robin!" he shouted back, as he scratched and clawed desperately against the side of the dish like a man sinking in quicksand. Then he disappeared into the depths of the water without another sound.

There was a long, eerie silence.

Suddenly, like a volcanic explosion, the Cable Guy burst out of the water, holding Steven above his head like a psychotic wrestler as he moved in victorious slow-motion.

Robin gasped and covered her mouth with both hands. "Steven!"

"WWF, World Wrestling Federation BACK-BREAK-ER!" the Cable Guy announced, and then slammed Steven down onto his knee.

There was an audible snap. Stunned and semiconscious, Steven rolled off to the edge of the water.

"Boom Bam!" the Cable Guy shouted.

Then, still moving in his own slow-motion, like the conquering warrior he believed that he was, the Cable Guy walked toward Robin.

"Da-da-da," he sang dramatically, holding his arms out wide and imitating the majestic power of a full orchestra playing martial music. "Da-da-da!"

Then he grabbed Robin around the neck and held a staple gun to her head.

"Don't try anything funny," he warned her.

She nodded, and raised her hands to indicate that she would go with him quietly and cooperatively. Being stapled would be a nasty fate.

"Let's get going," he said, and then forced her to walk up to the edge of the dish.

Lying on his back in a stupor, Steven opened his eyes. At first, he had trouble focusing, but then he saw that the Cable Guy and Robin were beginning to climb up the hundred-foot-tall radio antenna.

What was she thinking; she *hated* heights?!

He shook his head, trying to blast away the cobwebs of unconsciousness, and then finally figured out that she wasn't going willingly.

He got up, groaning from the pain of various bumps and strains, and headed after them.

Far above him, the Cable Guy and Robin made steady progress as they climbed the radio antenna.

"This is, um, kind of high," Robin said at one point, her voice close to hysteria.

"Well, of course it is. The better to receive signals from throughout the world," the Cable Guy explained helpfully. "Now *move!*"

Robin kept climbing as Steven followed them from a distance, trying to keep out of sight.

Finally, she and the Cable Guy reached a small platform at the top of the antenna. It was swaying in the wind, and Robin shut her eyes, so that she wouldn't—not even for a second— catch a glimpse of the view.

The Cable Guy gripped Robin's arm tightly

with one hand and pressed the staple gun against her right temple with the other.

Just then, Steven scrambled up onto the platform, breathing hard from his climb.

"Easy," he said, holding his hands out. "Come on, take it easy."

The Cable Guy forced Robin to walk over to the end of the platform. There was a hundred-foot drop to the satellite dish below them.

"Come on," Steven said, very calm. "Just take it—"

"You know, it really didn't have to be this way, Steven," the Cable Guy answered him sadly as he gazed down at the yawning expanse of the satellite dish. "I'm just trying to show you the kind of things that can happen when you mistreat people."

"Why are we up here?" Steven asked, going out of his way to sound pleasant. "Do you have a plan?"

The Cable Guy thought about that. "No, I'm pretty much going moment to moment," he said. "Winging it, really. But hey, you've got to admit this is a pretty cool place for an ending."

Steven shook his head, confused. "Ending to what?"

"*You* know," the Cable Guy said enthusiastically, his eyes bright with excitement. "This is just like that movie, *Goldeneye*—"

"No!" Steven yelled. "This is not like *any-thing*. This isn't a movie, this is reality! Don't you get it? You're *hurting* us!"

This remark hit the Cable Guy like a sucker punch, and his eyes turned sad again. Looking dazed, he let go of Robin and she ran across the platform into Steven's welcoming arms.

From the ground below the dish, a helicopter was rising into the air until it was hovering next to the tower. The Cable Guy gazed at the chopper, looked down at the drop, and then turned his attention to Steven.

"I just wanted to be your friend," he said, crushed by his failure. "But I guess I messed it up."

Someone inside the hovering helicopter shined a bright spotlight directly in the Cable Guy's eyes. He stared into the light and nodded his head as if the light were sending him a heavenly message.

"What's that?" he asked in a hushed voice. He listened, and then nodded again. "Huh? Come again?" He listened. "Oh, I see. You want me to quiet down and just chill out in front of the TV for a while." He scowled at nothing. "You were never there for me, were you, Mother? You expected Mike and Carol Brady to raise me, with a little help from Hazel and Mr. Eddie's father." He flung his arms out to the side. "I am the natural son of Claire

Huxtable! I am the lost Cunningham! I learned the facts of life by *watching The Facts of Life*!" He hung his head in shame. "That's it! That's really it!"

With that, the Cable Guy climbed up onto the railing surrounding the platform, getting ready to jump off into oblivion.

Below them, sirens were blaring as a stream of police cars pulled up to surround the satellite dish.

"Don't do it," Steven begged. "Come down. We'll all go out." He racked his brain, wanting to come up with something irresistible. "We'll—have a drink together!"

"I'm not thirsty anymore," the Cable Guy said with a gentle smile. "See ya." He pushed himself up until he was standing precariously on the railing. "I have a purpose now!"

"No!" Steven said, and he rushed forward to try and stop him from jumping.

Before he got there, the Cable Guy toppled backwards off the rail. Steven dove towards him and reached his hand out past the rail. He managed to grab the Cable Guy's forearm just as he completed a free-falling backflip.

"You're not going anywhere," Steven said firmly, as he hung onto the antenna with his other hand so that the Cable Guy's weight wouldn't drag him off the platform.

The Cable Guy didn't answer, swinging

back and forth, high above the satellite dish.

Steven gritted his teeth and used all of his strength to try and pull him back onto the platform, but the Cable Guy did not want to be saved.

"Don't do this," Steven pleaded. "You just need help. We all get lonely."

"Yeah, but I get *really* lonely," the Cable Guy said. Then he grinned bashfully. "I mean, look at me. C'mon."

"You're gonna be fine," Steven promised, hanging on with all of his might. "Just come on up."

The Cable Guy didn't answer for a long beat. "Steven, I think I sat too close to the television," he said finally. "Mommy was right."

His dead weight was so heavy that Steven couldn't hold onto his forearm any longer. The Cable Guy's arm slipped, but with a superhuman effort, Steven was able to grab his hand at the last possible second.

"Come on!" Steven shouted. "Hang on!"

"No, it's too late for me," the Cable Guy said, "but there's a lot of little Cable Boys out there who still have a chance." He smiled wistfully at the thought, then reached over to hold onto Steven with both hands. He pulled himself up so that he could speak directly into Steven's face. "Don't you see, Steven? Somebody has to kill the babysitter."

With those enigmatic words, he let go of Steven's hand and began falling backwards toward the dish below.

All over the city, people were gathered around their television sets, doing their best to be part of the global community. In a nearby suburban home, a nuclear family sat in a row on the couch, watching Court TV.

A reporter was speaking to the camera from the familiar courthouse where the Sam Sweet trial had been going on for so many weeks.

"*This* is the moment America has been waiting for," the reporter said, barely able to contain his complete exhilaration. "We've just been told that the jury is ready to render their decision."

The family leaned closer to the television set, holding their breaths.

Up above the satellite dish, the Cable Guy sailed through the air. As he fell, he looked almost peaceful, appearing to be totally comfortable with what he was doing.

At the same moment, across town, a couch potato lounged on the fold-out bed in his apartment, his eyes glued to the television.

The camera had switched inside the courtroom, where a court clerk was about to read the jury's decision.

"By unanimous vote," she started, "the defendant, Sam Sweet . . ."

The Cable Guy plummeted endlessly towards the satellite dish, about to hit the bottom.

Meanwhile, in a local neighborhood bar, a crowd of revelers had gathered around the television in total silence. They had been waiting for this verdict for a very long time.

". . . has been found . . ." the court clerk was saying.

At that very moment, the Cable Guy landed in the satellite dish with a heavy thud, and the reception on every single television in the greater metropolitan area instantly turned to white noise.

Realizing that they weren't going to hear the verdict, a collective scream of anguish and despair rose up all over the wide panorama of the city, echoing through the dark night.

All of the televisions in the entire city had simultaneously gone . . . *dead*.

From up on top of the radio antenna, Steven and Robin gasped when they saw the Cable

Guy's silhouette lying motionless on the struts of the satellite dish.

It was the most horrible thing either of them had ever seen.

Down at the bottom of the dish, it appeared as though the needle of the antenna had impaled the Cable Guy. Either way, it was clear that the satellite dish's vital mechanisms had been destroyed, eliminating television signals for miles around.

The Cable Guy opened his eyes and looked at the lethally sharp metal needle poking out between his arm and his rib cage.

"Close one," he observed, and then passed out.

Back in the couch potato's apartment, he stared at the white noise, not sure what to do. He watched so much television that his skin was pasty white from never seeing the sun. In his whole life, the only thing he had ever done in his free time was to watch endless, mind-numbing hours of television.

*Now* what was he supposed to do?!

He sat on the edge of his fold-out bed, utterly at a loss. How would he fill his days? How would he fill the next five minutes? His life was an empty shell.

Then his expression cheered up a little, and

he reached out a tentative hand to pick up . . . a book. He held it for a moment, very unsure of himself, and then slowly opened the cover and began to *read*.

It was a whole new world.

When everyone realized that the Cable Guy was badly injured but still alive, there was a flurry of activity around the satellite dish. Rescue workers scrambled down inside the dish with a stretcher and carried him tenderly out to the waiting emergency helicopter.

Steven and Robin watched all of this, wrapped up in heavy wool police blankets someone had handed them.

As the Cable Guy was carried past them, Steven put his hand out to stop the stretcher.

The Cable Guy smiled weakly at them. "You two are going to do just fine," he said.

Steven picked up his hand and clasped it warmly. "You never told me your real name."

"You really want to know my real name?" the Cable Guy asked, delighted. "It's . . . Richard Ricardo. But my friends call me Ricky." He laughed. "Ricky Ricardo, get it?" Then he slumped back down on the stretcher, losing strength. "I'm just messing with ya."

The paramedics put him on the helicopter and then slapped the fuselage twice so that the pilot would know it was safe to take off.

Steven and Robin held each other close, and watched as the helicopter grew smaller and smaller in the night sky, and finally flew out of sight.

"Let's go home," Robin whispered.

They kissed gently and turned to walk to the car.

Maybe they would never know his name, but they would never forget him either.

One of the paramedics was accompanying the Cable Guy on his flight to the nearest trauma center, and he carefully checked his patient's vital signs. The Cable Guy lay on his stretcher, barely conscious, struggling for survival.

"Hang in there, buddy," the paramedic said in a low, comforting voice. He gave the Cable Guy's shoulder a light pat. "Come on, stay with me. Just stay with me."

The Cable Guy's eyes fluttered open and he lifted a weak hand to motion for the paramedic to come closer. He might be fighting for life, but right now, his eyes were dancing with excitement. Against all odds, he had found a reason to live.

"Am I *really* your buddy?" he asked sweetly.